Dare to collect them all!

More books from The Midnight Library:
Nick Shadow's terrifying collection continues . . .

Voices

Blood and Sand

End Game

The Cat Lady

Shut Your Mouth

I Can See You

The Catch

THE MIDNIGHT LIBRARY

Liar

Nick Shadow

Hodder Children's Books
A division of Hachette Children's Books

Special thanks to Tina Barrett

Created by Working Partners Limited, London W6 0QT

First published in Great Britain in 2006
by Hodder Children's Books

2

A Catalogue record for this book is available from the British Library

ISBN-10: 0 340 89409 1
ISBN-13: 9780340894095

Typeset in Weiss Antiqua by Avon DataSet Ltd,
Bidford-on-Avon, Warwickshire

Printed and bound in Great Britain by
Clays Ltd, St Ives plc

The paper and board used in this paperback by Hodder Children's Books are natural recyclable products made from wood grown in sustainable forests. The manufacturing processes conform to the environmental regulations of the country of origin.

Hodder Children's Books
a division of Hachette Children's Books
338 Euston Road
London NW1 3BH

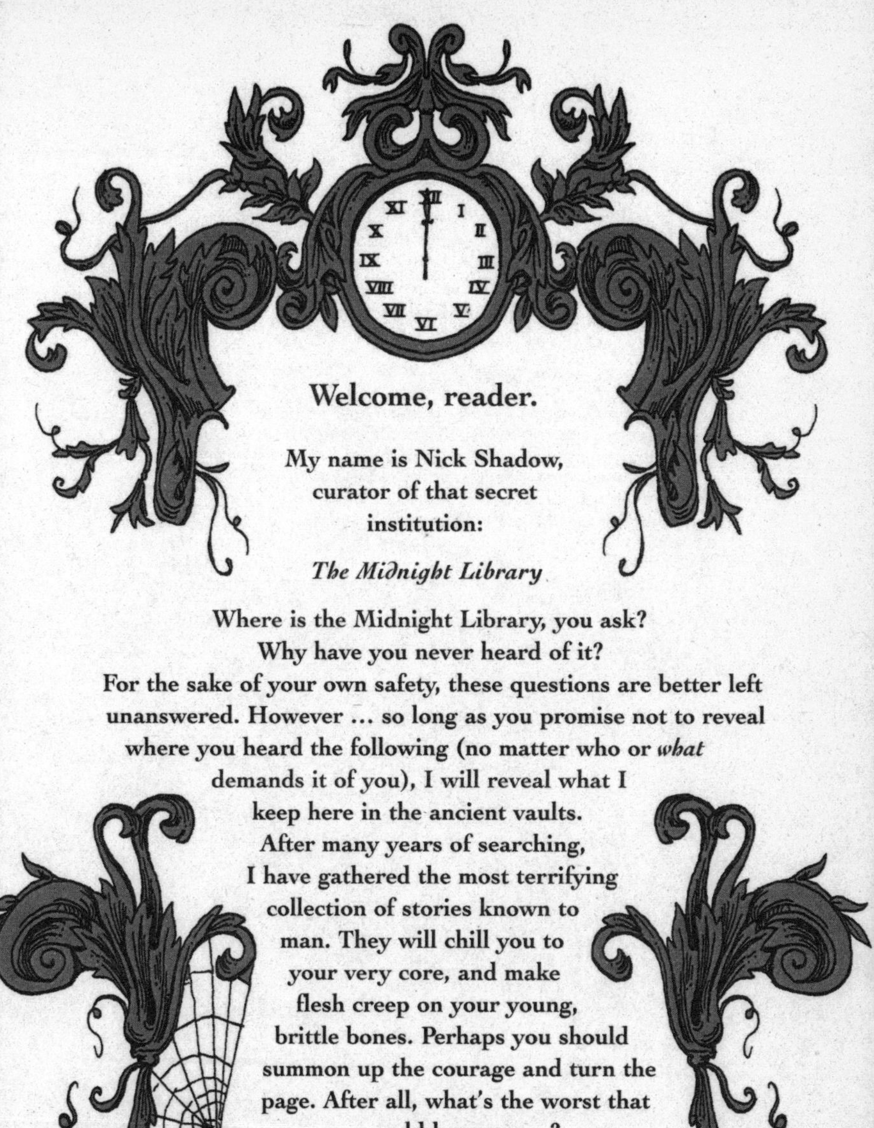

Welcome, reader.

My name is Nick Shadow,
curator of that secret
institution:

The Midnight Library

Where is the Midnight Library, you ask?
Why have you never heard of it?
For the sake of your own safety, these questions are better left unanswered. However ... so long as you promise not to reveal where you heard the following (no matter who or *what* demands it of you), I will reveal what I keep here in the ancient vaults. After many years of searching, I have gathered the most terrifying collection of stories known to man. They will chill you to your very core, and make flesh creep on your young, brittle bones. Perhaps you should summon up the courage and turn the page. After all, what's the worst that could happen ... ?

The Midnight Library: Volume V

Stories by Tina Barrett

CONTENTS

LIAR

Lauren Wolfe pressed her forehead against the glass of the bus window. It was cold and hard against her skin, and she felt every bump and jolt of the short journey home from school. She was seated alone as usual, the rest of her classmates gathered in comfortable groups along the walkway, chatting and laughing easily together. She was thirteen today, and not a single person had wished her 'Happy Birthday'.

Through the rain-spattered pane, she watched a

young mum push a pram along the high street. She was suddenly grateful for her warm seat inside the bus as the stream of cars and buses sailed straight past the woman and the baby, soaking them with spray. Lauren pulled her head away in shock as the woman crossed in front of them without looking, shoving herself and the pram into the road. The cars skidded to a shuddering halt and Lauren cried out in alarm as the bus-driver slammed on his brakes, throwing everyone perilously forward in their seats.

'Take it easy, driver!' yelled a boy from the back seat.

Lauren managed to steady herself by grabbing the steel rail attached to the driver's booth. She could hear other passengers complaining behind her as they struggled to right themselves.

'Haven't you passed your test yet?' someone shouted at the driver.

'Probably didn't have driving tests when he was young,' teased someone else. 'Only horses.'

Everyone laughed, including Lauren. She looked

around for someone to share the joke with but found no one. *Friends will come*, she told herself, with a sigh. *You've only been at this school for two weeks. Things will be different here, you'll see.*

As the driver pulled away again, she pressed her head against the window once more just to feel the coldness of the glass beneath her skin and to reassure herself that she really did exist.

The bus rattled on, its doors spitting out passengers along the route with a snake-like hiss. Behind Lauren, noisy chatter turned to squeals and shrieks and Lauren strained to hear what her classmates were laughing about. Lauren hated the fact that she was so shy. She felt tears prick her eyes, and immediately clawed them back. She had always felt crippled by her shyness. At her last school, it had gripped her so tightly that Lauren had eventually given up trying to make friends, settling instead for becoming wallpaper. Wallpaper, she realized, just hung in the background, largely unnoticed by anyone. It was a lonely existence, but she reasoned that it was better than being laughed at.

For the next two stops, Lauren eavesdropped silently from behind the headrest. She listened to a bunch of girls from her class who were sitting near the back and chatting eagerly about clothes and shopping. She had a fair idea of the names of most of these girls, especially the one that was talking the most – her name was Chantelle, and she was *cool*. She had effortless-looking dark hair and startling blue eyes. And she always seemed to accessorize her school clothes with the coolest stuff.

'Wicked hoop earrings, with rhinestones round the rim . . . dead cheap from Trend in the high street,' said Chantelle. Lauren watched the others huddle round and admire her new accessories with loud *oohs* and *aahs*.

She felt her own earlobes; they were bare. She never wore earrings – or any jewellery for that matter. Fashion wasn't something Lauren knew that much about. She felt her cheeks burn with jealousy.

She wondered what it felt like to be confident, to be the centre of attention and to have all your classmates surrounding you, giving you admiring glances and compliments. She bet it felt good.

And then it happened. Lauren had been so lost in her own thoughts that she hadn't noticed somebody sit down next to her. But this 'somebody' wasn't just anybody. It was a boy. In fact, he was the cutest-looking boy Lauren had *ever* seen.

The boy smiled at her, a wide, friendly kind of smile. 'You're the new girl, aren't you? Laura, isn't it?'

He had a pair of huge toffee-brown eyes and unruly dark curls that flopped arrestingly over his forehead. Lauren tried to stop staring like an idiot and concentrate on what he was saying.

She struggled to reply. 'I . . . I'm . . . erm . . . I mean . . . hi.' She kicked herself for sounding like a complete klutz. She'd wanted to say *Hi! Actually, my name's Lauren, not Laura, but it's really nice to meet you.* But instead, she just found herself smiling like a loon.

'Well, anyway, my name's Marcus Hodges.'

Lauren watched as Marcus made his way back along the aisle. What she wouldn't give to have a boyfriend like that!

For a moment, Lauren allowed herself to consider it, and her heart fluttered. Well, he had sat next to her, hadn't he? And he had known her name too! OK, so he had called her 'Laura' instead of 'Lauren' – but it was a start. At least he had noticed her. Her cheeks flushed hot at the thought and a grin spread across her face. Perhaps things *would* be different here after all. Her birthday was beginning to look up.

Lauren glanced around the edge of her seat, but immediately wished she hadn't. Marcus was standing right beside Chantelle and they were so close the tips of their noses almost touched. She was giggling and smiling whilst he tied a scarf around her neck, passing a hand over her new round earrings.

Lauren burned with embarrassment. How *stupid* she was to think that a boy like Marcus would ever be interested in someone like *her*. She reached for her schoolbag as the bus drew close to her stop. Standing at the doors, she gave Marcus and Chantelle a final glance. They were still standing close, wrapped up in their own little world. As Lauren stepped off the bus, she was suddenly cross. For the first time since she could remember, she was fed up with being wallpaper.

I am not going to be invisible any more! she vowed as she marched up the street towards home.

As she walked home in the rain, Lauren knew that it was *definitely* a chocolate day. Chocolate was always a friend when life was rubbish. Lauren headed for the newsagent's on the corner of her road, pushing open the door, searching out change in her purse.

Inside, row upon row of bright coloured wrappers stretched out enticingly before her, and Lauren studied them all in search of the one she wanted. Eventually, she picked a milk chocolate bar in a large size.

'Better be careful – you'll get fat,' joked the man behind the counter, pointing at her skinny frame.

Lauren handed over the money. 'I'm treating myself,' she said, forcing a smile. 'It's my birthday.'

She ripped open the wrapper and broke off a chunk. Apart from earlier with Marcus on the bus, Lauren realized that nobody had spoken to her all day. *Maybe this is how every birthday will be*, she thought miserably, as she bit into the chocolate.

'Ooh, you've a face on you to curdle milk,' laughed the man. 'You'd never think you're celebrating today.'

'I'm sorry, what?' said Lauren, not understanding what the man meant.

'Aren't you having a party?' His face was all smiles.

The chocolate stuck in Lauren's throat. She had nothing like that planned. In fact, she didn't even know if her parents would be there when she got home. They were always working late.

'You *are* having a party, aren't you?' the newsagent asked, when Lauren didn't reply.

'Me? Oh yes, of course I am.' She forced a smile.

The newsagent put a large pile of glossy-looking magazines in a plastic carrier bag, and handed them to Lauren. 'Well, here's a little something from me, anyway. They're only back issues, but you can share them with all your friends.'

Lauren smiled. She was really touched by the man's kindness, but the fact that only a stranger had bothered to wish her a happy birthday today only made matters worse. She felt the muscles in her cheeks twitch, and she knew that was the first sign of tears.

'Thanks for these,' she said quietly. 'I think I'd better take another chocolate bar before I go.'

As she had suspected, the house was empty when Lauren returned, but she didn't actually mind as much as she thought she would. She walked into the kitchen and found a pile of cards on the table. She picked up the envelopes, recognizing all the different handwriting – all cousins and aunts and uncles. It was nice, but not as nice as if she had got some cards from her friends. Then Lauren heard the front door open.

'Hello? Birthday girl!' her father called out.

'Dad!' Lauren called, running into the hallway and giving her dad a big hug.

'I wanted to get back early for your birthday, but the traffic was murder. Sorry about that.'

'That's fine,' Lauren said, not letting her dad go.

'You OK, darling?' he said, concern clouding his features.

'I'm all right now, Dad – it's just nice to see you,' Lauren replied.

'Come and see what your mum and I got you!'

Her face split into a grin. This was more like it!

'Thirteen today, Lol,' he said, planting a kiss on top of her head. 'You'll soon be old enough to vote.'

'I'll be able to drive a car first!' she laughed.

Lauren covered her eyes with her hands, and her dad led her down the hall towards the front room.

The front door slammed again. 'Only me,' called

her mother. 'The traffic's murder tonight. Have you started without me? No peeping yet,' she teased. 'Not till we tell you to.'

Lauren heard the sound of plastic bags rustling and boxes opening. She could barely contain her excitement. 'Hurry up,' she urged.

'OK, then,' said her dad, removing her hands from her eyes. 'You can open them now.'

There in front of her on the dining-room table was a brand new computer.

Lauren gasped in delight. 'Is that for me?'

'Yes, it is,' said her mother. 'You can put it in your room.'

'It's got a flat screen, remote-controlled mouse plus broadband Internet connection,' said her dad, ever the computer nut.

'It's the best present ever,' Lauren said happily. 'Can we set it up?'

'First things first,' said her mother, 'I've got your favourite for dinner – Chinese!'

Lauren beamed. It was turning out to be quite a

good birthday after all – until conversation across the dinner table turned to school.

'Good day?' her mother asked over a prawn cracker.

'Great,' Lauren lied.

'You could have invited a friend over if you'd wanted to,' her mother ventured.

'I know,' said Lauren, not looking up from her plate. She felt her face go red. How could she explain she didn't actually have any friends to invite over? Her father came to the rescue.

'Darling, this *is* Lauren we're talking about,' he said, giving her a wink. 'She's far too busy with schoolwork for that kind of thing. In fact,' Dad began in his changing-the-subject voice, 'I was talking to a colleague at work today. He's got a daughter in Lauren's class. I think she's called Chanteuse or Canterelle or something . . .'

'Chantelle,' corrected Lauren.

'That's the one! Well – apparently he's got the devil's job with her. She's always on the Internet, chatting on those message boards. Her grades are plummeting, and she never gets any schoolwork done.'

'You won't do that, will you, Lauren?' her mum said, anxiously.

'I didn't mean that Lauren—' her dad began.

'Of course I won't, Mum,' Lauren replied, cutting her father off mid-sentence. Lauren's favourite noodles suddenly tasted like straw. If her father had meant to cheer her up, he had failed miserably. She tried to eat the rest of her dinner, but her appetite had disappeared.

'Can we set my computer up now, Dad?' she asked, anxious to leave the table and the conversation.

Lauren watched her dad fire a look of concern at her mum. 'I'll be with you in a couple of minutes, Lol – why don't you go into the lounge and watch some TV?'

Lauren excused herself and slumped down on the sofa. She could feel a tiny flame of desire ignite inside her.

She wanted to be one of the girls at the centre of the chat in a chat room.

She wanted to know about music and clothes.

As Lauren let the TV programme wash over her, she knew that she was most of all sick to death of knowing about algebra and angles and boring stuff that never seemed to help her, ever.

A little while later, Lauren was sitting at the desk in her bedroom, the computer connected and ready to boot up. She gave her dad a kiss. 'Thanks. I love my present,' she said. 'It's brilliant.'

'If you need any help,' he said, disappearing round the bedroom door, 'just give me a shout.' Before he left, he reached inside his jacket and got out his credit card. 'Get yourself some books with this, if you like. Happy birthday, love.'

'Thanks, Dad!' Lauren replied.

Lauren flicked the switch and the monitor burst into life. She grinned in anticipation. A computer was something she'd been nagging her parents to buy her for over a year now. Quickly, she connected to the Internet and then sat back. *Where should I go first?* Without really thinking, she reached for the keyboard and typed in the search 'pop music'.

Thousands of listings flashed up in front of her, and she suddenly felt swamped. What was the name of the band that she had heard the girls talking about that day at school? She wanted to buy some music, not some more books. Her hand hovered uncertainly over the mouse. The trouble was that Lauren wasn't absolutely sure what the band were called. What if she bought the wrong CDs?

Suddenly, Lauren had a brainwave. The magazines that the man in the shop had given her! There *had* to be some information in those that could help her out. And sure enough, after only a moment's searching, she found a feature called *'In and Out – what's hot and what's not! A need-to-know guide.'*

Lauren studied it intently. Written beneath the 'In' column was a list of all the things currently in fashion while beneath the 'Out' column were all the things going out of fashion.

Apparently, rhinestone hoop earrings were currently out of fashion. Lauren couldn't help a secret smile to herself at that piece of information.

Underneath the 'In' column she read that ballerina shoes, denim skirts and beanie hats were the *must-have* clothes items at the moment. Red lipstick was out whilst pink lip-gloss was in. At last she came to the bit she was looking for, the music section. According to *Teen Power* and confirmed by *Girl Spirit*, Scum were on the way out and The Chinchillas were the new band on the block, mainly because of their super-cool lead singer, Luke Skyler.

Lauren picked up her dad's credit card. The Chinchillas' album stared enticingly at her from the screen. Before she could change her mind, Lauren was clicking the CD into her shopping cart, and when the prompt came up, she began typing the number of the credit card into the secure server.

The payment screen came up immediately. *'Thank*

you for shopping. Your purchase will be despatched immediately. Please click here to continue shopping.'

Now that her dad's credit card details were stored on the website, Lauren found herself ordering two more CDs recommended in one of the magazines. After signing off, she found herself completely absorbed by the teen gossip and beauty articles. There was a section entirely dedicated to the best online message forums. Apparently, lots of the kids at school were logging on to them during IT lessons. As a result, they had become banned during school hours. Lauren had heard some of the kids from her class discussing a particular chat room called The Outer Zone. Apparently it had loads of cool stuff that went on in their area, and so was mostly occupied by users from her school and the neighbouring town's schools.

Lauren's mind wandered. She wondered if Marcus Hodges chatted on The Outer Zone. Suddenly, she was seized by a sudden urge to go online and find out. She only had to tap in the chat room web address. A surge of excitement rushed through her as she considered what she would do if Marcus really *did* use the site. Perhaps, she could get to know him through the forum. At least online, her tongue wouldn't tie itself up in knots.

The thought spurred her on, and before she could stop herself she had tapped in the address on her browser. Her finger hovered nervously above the mouse button. She was only a click away, when she heard her father's voice from the foot of the stairs. 'Have you found anything you like, Lauren?'

Lauren closed down the screen immediately. 'Er . . . yes thanks, Dad!' she called down.

She closed her new PC down and got changed for bed – but she wasn't tired at all. She was thinking hard. *If I'm going to stop being invisible*, she thought, *then I'll make sure I'm noticed for all the right reasons*. She got into bed with a pile of the magazines next to her. Next time she logged on to The Outer Zone, Lauren was determined to be prepared.

* * *

Over the next week, Lauren studied the magazines and websites for the latest music and fashion trends. She got her new CDs through the post, and actually really enjoyed them. She was beginning to feel confident in what she knew. When she wasn't doing that, she was listening to her classmates in the school canteen or on the bus ride home. In a bid to familiarize herself with the latest gossip, Lauren had started taking a seat halfway down the bus instead of her usual place in the front row. It was the perfect set-up for her to tune in to what was going on.

After a few days, Lauren made up her mind. Tonight would be the night she'd take the bull by the horns and venture into The Outer Zone.

When she'd finished supper, Lauren went to her bedroom and booted up her computer. As she waited nervously for it to load, she put on one of her new CDs and turned up the volume. Within seconds, screaming guitar riffs filled her bedroom, and suddenly, The Outer Zone was on her screen. Bright neon colours glared out at her from a purple background and Lauren blinked her eyes, trying to find her bearings on the page. At the top of the screen, a bright banner welcomed her. *'The Outer Zone Message Forum,'* it read. *'Out there for teenagers everywhere.'*

Underneath, images of perfect-looking teenagers all dressed in the latest fashions seemed to be chatting and laughing together. *'Welcome to the coolest forum in Cyberspace,'* said a tag line underneath. *'Hot chat topics on this site today are:* ***Celebrity Gossip, Pop Music, Chit Chat, Fashion and Beauty.***'

Just then, she noticed a link at the top of the page. *'Welcome Newcomer,'* it read. *'Why not sign in as a guest to visit this forum? Click here to begin!'*

It was just what she needed. She clicked the link gratefully.

'Thank you, guest,' flashed up the reply. *'You are now logged in and can leave messages on any of The Outer Zone's boards.'*

The screen changed and the 'Pop Music' Message Board welcomed her. To Lauren's frustration though, she found she had even more choices to make.

'Threads in Pop Music,' announced the banner and below it was another list.

'This is so complicated,' she said to herself. Her eyes searched down the screen at the various categories for discussion. *'Goth talk,' 'Death of Scum,' 'Rap,' 'Garage,' 'Street . . .'* There was nothing here Lauren knew anything about, but just as she was going to go to another topic, she saw a discussion topic called *'The Rise of The Chinchillas.'*

'Finally, a band that I know something about,' she smiled to herself.

A long list of messages about The Chinchillas scrolled down the screen with a 'reply' button beside each one in case anybody had a comment or reply to make.

'Luke Skyler of The Chinchillas is so fit!' read one of the messages.

'Has anybody met him?' wrote someone called 'ChanD'. Lauren felt a jolt of worry go through her. Could that be Chantelle? After all, her surname was Dawson.

Next, Lauren scanned the long list of people who had left posts to try to work out if any of the screen names could belong to Marcus. Lauren felt a little dejected – there didn't seem to be any screen names resembling Marcus Hodges. Eventually, she found a link that told her which members were currently logged on to the forum. She recognized some of the screen names such as ChanD for Chantelle Dawson, and JoC for Chantelle's best friend Josie Culver, but there was nobody online whose screen name seemed to match Marcus.

She was all set to log off when curiosity got the better of her. She found herself clicking the 'reply' button to Chantelle's question about Luke Skyler, lead singer of The Chinchillas.

It wouldn't hurt to reply, she thought. *After all, I'm signed in as Guest. Nobody knows who I am*. She began to type.

'I haven't actually met Luke Skyler,' she began, *'but I do know quite a bit of stuff about him.'*

With a deep breath, Lauren hit the 'send' button.

Immediately, she saw her message flash up with

the screen name 'Guest' beside it. She felt breathless excitement – she'd done it! She wondered if Chantelle would even bother to answer, but almost immediately, a reply came back.

'Hi Guest,' Chantelle had written. *'Tell me everything.'*

Lauren grinned, immediately pleased she had taken the risk. It was a good job she'd read Luke Skyler's profile in *Pow* magazine this morning.

'Well – I know he's a Gemini and that his birthday's June 12th. His fave food is French fries and he was born in Amsterdam.'

She hit the 'send' button and waited for a reply. It didn't take long. She definitely had Chantelle's attention now.

'Cool,' came the reply. *'I luv fries too. He's such a babe. We have soooo much in common. What else do you know? BTW, who are you, Guest?'*

The last question rooted Lauren to her chair. She was now on the spot. Was she was ready to reveal herself yet?

Panicking slightly, she took a moment to compose

her answer. *'It doesn't matter who I am,'* Lauren wrote back. *'I'm a massive Chinchillas fan, just like you.'* She tried to change the subject. *'Their new album is terrific, especially the song called "You're Gone". It's got a brilliant instrumental bit at the end where the violins go really staccato.'*

But as soon as she'd hit the 'reply' button she knew she'd made a mistake. Back came the reply within seconds: *'Violins? Are U having a laugh?'*

Lauren's palms were drenched with sweat. Nobody her age discussed classical instruments! They talked about guitar riffs, cool lead singers and earrings. She was out of her depth and drowning fast. She had to fix her mistake.

'Only joking,' she typed. *'Did you know Luke Skyler's favourite colour is purple?'*

'Everybody knows that,' came back the response from ChanD. Then another one in quick succession. *'Tell us who you are, 'Guest' – we don't appreciate uninvited visitors on our board – especially those who try too hard to fit in. Come on – who are you?'*

Lauren was now really worried. She made a snap

decision, and began to type. *'I think that you might know me from the bus to school. My name's Lauren.'*

But it was too late. A reply reached her screen.

'I reckon I've sussed who U R!' it read. *'U R that geek girl who hides behind the seats spying on everyone. Only a loser like U would like classical music. Nice try on pretending to like The Chinchillas though – LOL!'*

Lauren's cheeks burned with shame as she watched other replies flashing up thick and fast.

'Laurentheloser!' read another message from ChanD.

'Y don't U get a life?' JoC's posting said.

'Get lost, looooooser!!!!!!' the final message from ChanD said.

'No!' she shouted to herself in frustration. Lauren sank back into her chair, tears prickling her eyes. Why did this have to happen? Her heart sank. She closed the screen and logged off. Those girls would never be friends with her now. The only comfort Lauren felt was, as far as she could tell, Marcus hadn't been online tonight to see her humiliated.

With any luck he would never find out.

* * *

But Lauren was wrong. When she arrived at school the next morning people began to point at her and laugh. It seemed that Chantelle had made sure to tell everyone.

'Oh look,' Chantelle said as Lauren took her place in registration. 'Here comes the Guest! Pity she's an unwanted one!'

Everybody laughed, including Marcus, and Lauren felt just as if she had been thumped in the chest. Why couldn't she have just stuck to being anonymous? She was the centre of attention now, but not for any of the reasons she'd wanted.

'What did you expect, Laura?' Marcus said. 'You should have just been yourself, instead of trying to hide. That would have been enough.'

Lauren felt more mixed up and confused than ever as she watched him walk away. Be herself? Lauren hadn't even thought of that. Well maybe, just maybe, it was worth a try!

* * *

That night, spurred on by Marcus's words, Lauren decided to have another go. She signed on once more to The Outer Zone. This time she decided to make it clear who she was. She took the screen name 'UnwantedGuest'. Lauren was determined to do exactly as Marcus said, and talk to the others without hiding.

She found her classmates chatting in the 'Chit Chat' zone and decided to start a new thread.

'Hi Guys,' she wrote. *'It's the unwanted guest! Sorry about last night. Does anybody want to chat?'*

Lauren saw her message flash up on the screen and waited.

Five minutes passed.

Then ten. Nobody replied.

Perhaps they're all having their dinner, Lauren thought hopefully. She clicked the link showing current members still active in The Outer Zone, and her hopes sank. They were all still online. They just weren't posting on Lauren's thread.

Lauren gave it a final shot.

'Realize you must all be annoyed about last night but I'm really sorry. Can we chat?' she typed, her fingers trembling slightly.

Fifteen more minutes passed with no replies. She felt bitterness and anger welling up inside her. What was it Marcus had said? She should be herself, and that would be enough. Well, the message board told her otherwise.

Being herself was *not* enough.

Chantelle and the others clearly didn't want to know Lauren, whether she was 'Guest' or herself. She logged off, feeling miserable. She slammed the mouse down on the desk and closed off her computer. Trying to make herself feel better, she put on The Chinchillas, but as the music began, she felt a wave of revulsion for it all, and jabbed the 'stop' button with her finger.

As she sat there, dejected, Lauren saw one of the magazines open nearby, and a beautiful model was staring up at her from the pages. 'If only I was you,' she told the girl on the page. 'Then everyone would want to know me.'

Lauren sat bolt upright. As soon as the words had left her mouth, an idea came into her head. She immediately knew what to do.

She sat down once more in front of her computer and waited impatiently for it to boot up. Once online, she logged straight back on to The Outer Zone. Clicking open the registration page, Lauren feverishly reworked her details. It was so obvious! Marcus had told Lauren to try being herself – but he had been wrong. All her life she had been herself and it had never been good enough. She began to search for her classmates on 'Chit Chat'.

If people didn't like Lauren for who she was, then the answer was to be someone *completely different*.

As she typed, a broad grin spread across Lauren's face. This was going to be fun.

'Hi guys, my name's Jennifer,' it read. *'And I've just met Luke Skyler from The Chinchillas. Does anyone want to chat?'*

* * *

Lauren was amazed how quickly the time flew by. So many people wanted to chat with 'Jennifer' that she didn't log off her computer until nearly midnight.

Chantelle had been the first to reply, demanding all the gossip about Jennifer's meeting with Luke Skyler. Lauren had hesitated slightly before typing in her first reply. She knew that everything that she typed in as Jennifer would have to be a lie, and Lauren didn't like lying. *But Jennifer's not real, so what's the problem?* she told herself, and began to type.

'I do a bit of modelling and bumped into The Chinchillas at one of my photo shoots. Luke Skyler was an absolute babe, even better than he looks in his photos. He was dead nice too, not stuck-up or anything. He even gave me a kiss and signed my T-shirt because I didn't have any paper.'

Lauren hit the 'send' button. As it flashed up on the screen, she reread it. It was such a fantastic lie that she couldn't believe anybody would buy it. But to her amazement and satisfaction, they did.

In fact, she had loads of replies to her message,

not just from Chantelle, but from Josie, plus at least a dozen other people from her school that she could recognize from their screen names. She read their comments with amazement.

'U lucky thing!'

'Do u think u could help me meet him?'

'Are u really a model?'

'How did you get to be a model?'

'Which designers do U model for?'

Lauren laughed at the last one. She didn't imagine anyone would *really* believe Jennifer was a model. She flicked through her magazines to see if she could find suitable inspiration for her reply.

'I was spotted in the street by a top agency. I have modelled loads, for Calvin Klein and loads of others. But modelling is very boring. When I leave school I want to go to art college. But I am also captain of my school hockey team and an Olympic coach has suggested I try out for the squad when I turn sixteen. It's dead hard to make a decision. What would u do?'

Lauren hit 'send', and realized that she had a wide

smile on her face. This was as happy as she'd felt in a long time. She was in control, and she was the centre of attention. And, more importantly, everyone – including Chantelle and Josie – seemed to think that she was cool.

But then she reread her last post. It seemed ridiculous to her – over the top and flimsy. Surely someone would challenge her? For a nervous minute, she waited for the screen to refresh itself.

'I would be a model,' answered Josie.

'Most definitely,' replied ChanD. *'Be a model!'*

For the next few days when she got home from school, Lauren pretended that she was going straight upstairs to do her homework, but she was actually creating the world that Jennifer lived in. She wanted to make sure that every part of her imaginary life was covered.

By day, Lauren was still the quiet and mostly ignored girl at school, but at night, she became Jennifer – a super-cool model with beautiful, long blonde hair and a great figure. When she was Jennifer, Lauren felt glamorous and envied.

And then on tonight's forum, a new member arrived. And the name stopped Lauren's heart for a second. She was sure it was Marcus Hodges.

'Hi Jen,' MarcH wrote.

Lauren took a deep breath. *'Hi there, MarcH!'* she replied.

They began to talk about a new film that she hadn't seen, but she'd read a few reviews of it online.

'So glad I'm not the only movie nut!' MarcH replied.

'Sequels r usually rubbish,' Lauren wrote, *'but this one was saved by the great acting.'*

'You are TOTALLY right!' MarcH replied.

Lauren couldn't believe how well she and Marcus were getting on! *Well*, she reminded herself, *it's Marcus and Jennifer that are getting along this well.*

The next day, Lauren was in the canteen eating her sandwich, and Marcus, Chantelle and Josie sat down on the table next to hers.

The talk turned to movies, and Lauren listened in as Marcus told the others about the film that she and he had talked about the night before.

'The effects were brilliant,' he was telling the others. 'You should go and see it.'

A friend of Marcus's called Aidan came and sat down with them. 'What's going on? What are you talking about, Marcus?' he said, grabbing a doughnut off Josie's tray and stuffing it into his mouth.

'That film I went to see, remember?' Marcus replied.

'But it's got a fifteen certificate. How did you get in?' Josie asked.

'I winged it,' grinned Marcus.

'Yes, but you look much older than us, Marcus,' said Chantelle, smiling coyly.

Lauren hated the way that Chantelle pandered to Marcus. But to Lauren's surprise, Marcus barely reacted. 'Thanks, Chan, but as I was saying, the effects were brilliant. In one of the scenes, the main character tumbles right off a cliff still clinging to the back of his horse and amazingly . . .'

'. . . they land at the bottom, completely untouched, and then ride off into battle and save the Grail,' Lauren finished.

Everyone on Marcus's table stopped and looked round to see who had just spoken. She was so caught up listening to the conversation, Lauren had inadvertently finished the sentence.

'That's right!' Marcus said. 'That's exactly right. And the main guy even . . .'

'. . . did his own stunts, apparently,' Lauren finished. She could feel Marcus watching her, and her cheeks began to burn.

Chantelle flashed her an angry look. 'How did you know that?'

'She must have seen it, of course,' answered Marcus. He turned to Lauren. 'That's right, isn't it?'

Lauren nodded, unable to think of a better reply. But it was clear to her that Chantelle wasn't buying it.

'Liar!' she sneered at Lauren. 'How could a geek like you blag your way into a fifteen certificate? You don't even look old enough for a Disney film!'

The comment stung Lauren, but instead of feeling like retreating into her shell, she felt something else – confidence. After all, Jennifer had told *much* bigger lies on The Outer Zone but Chantelle had been eager enough to swallow those. Lauren knew that it was only because she, and not Jennifer, had commented on the film that Chantelle was having a go at her. If Jennifer had done it, then there would have been no argument.

'Well, I did see the movie, as a matter of fact,' Lauren replied, staring at Chantelle hotly. 'My friend and I snuck in, and we watched it from the back.' She could feel Marcus's full attention on her, and it filled Lauren with confidence. 'But we were caught by the usher after about half an hour so we didn't manage to see the end.'

'Cool,' said Marcus, grinning. 'I can fill you in on the bits you missed if you like.' He got up to join her at the table but Chantelle grabbed his arm and dragged him back down.

'I wouldn't bother,' she said. 'It's all a pack of lies. I've never seen her with any friends, *ever*.'

'It's *not* a lie,' Lauren replied. She refused to let Chantelle ruin her moment in the spotlight.

Chantelle looked her straight in the eye. 'All right then, if you're telling the truth, then who is this mysterious friend of yours?'

Lauren felt sick with panic. What could she say? She saw Chantelle's eyes narrow, a glint of triumph in them.

'You wouldn't know her,' Lauren began. 'She doesn't go to this school.'

'Yeah right,' laughed Chantelle. 'That is *sooo* convenient.'

'It's not convenient,' replied Lauren in a level voice. 'It's true. We've been best friends for ages, but we only see each other at weekends now because my family moved towns and we have to time things when she's not on a modelling job.'

There was momentary silence as Chantelle eyed her suspiciously.

'Give her a break, Chan,' urged Marcus.

'I'll drop it once she's told me the name of this friend,' Chantelle persisted.

For a moment, Lauren toyed with the idea of walking away from it all, pretending that it never happened, consigning Jennifer to anonymity. But she couldn't. Looking around, she realized that she was now the centre of attention in real life, not just in a chat room. This was too good to give up for someone like Chantelle.

'Jennifer,' Lauren said without a flinch. 'My friend's name is Jennifer.'

For the rest of break, Marcus shared chips with Lauren and explained all the details of the end of the film that she and Jennifer had apparently missed. Lauren could barely hear what he was saying. She was too busy revelling in her victory over Chantelle, and happily enjoying sitting with the cutest boy in the school, whose full attention was on her.

When she returned home, Lauren felt like she was

floating. Everything had gone right for her . . . with a little bit of help from Jennifer.

That night, she logged on to The Outer Zone, signing in as Jennifer. It wasn't long before Marcus had found her, and began posting messages on her thread.

'Hi Jen,' he wrote. *'Got a question for u. U know you said you saw the film – Did u take a friend?'*

Lauren smiled to herself. *'Yes, I did,'* she replied. *'Why do u ask?'*

'Well, I was talking to a girl called Laura at school today. She said she snuck into the film with her friend Jennifer. I wondered if it was u, or am I barking up the wrong tree?'

Lauren felt a tingle of irritation. *'Her name is Lauren, actually,'* she typed. *'And yes, I did go with her. She's such a cool friend. We've known each other for years. My dad's a surgeon at a hospital and Lauren's mum's a medical researcher. We met at one of their boring hospital charity dos. Lauren was such a scream that she saved the whole day from turning into utter boresville, and we've been best mates ever since. UR so lucky she goes to your school. U should really get to know her.'*

Hopefully he'll want to talk to Lauren . . . I mean me, now! she thought. But to her dismay, Marcus's mind didn't seem to leave Jennifer.

His reply came back in an instant. *'It's U I'd really like to get to know, Jennifer. Y don't you send me your email address so we can talk off the forum and get to know each other better.'*

Lauren pushed away from the desk. Although she'd created a really great character in Jennifer, she hadn't bargained on *this* happening. It had been a simple enough matter changing her screen name to Jennifer so she could chat on The Outer Zone. But Lauren knew that she couldn't possibly give her own email address to Marcus. He'd suss everything out in flash and never speak to her again.

Marcus posted her again. *'Come on, Jen! What's taking so long?'*

In panic, Lauren typed in the first thing she could think of. *'Got to go. CUL8er!'*

She logged off, her heart beating fast. The lies were getting complicated now, and she didn't like having to trick someone as nice as Marcus. But on the other hand, Lauren had just had Marcus's undivided attention. Suddenly, the lies felt worth it.

The following morning, Lauren was just about to take her place for registration when she felt a gentle tap on her shoulder. She turned around and found herself face to face with Marcus. He looked a little nervous, and as he started to speak, Lauren thought that she heard him stammer slightly.

'Hi,' he said. 'I . . . er . . . I wondered if you've got a minute.'

Lauren blushed. She noticed Chantelle scowling furiously at her, but it was obvious she was jealous that Marcus was giving Lauren so much close attention. *Good old Jennifer,* thought Lauren. *Perhaps the good word she'd put in for Lauren last night had paid off after all!* 'Er, sure,' she said, 'what's up?'

Marcus took her arm and led her to a quiet corner of the classroom. 'I wanted you to have this,' he said, passing her a scrap of paper.

Lauren looked down. She read the blue scrawl. It was Marcus's email address. Lauren could hardly believe it. He'd considered all the nice things Jennifer had said about Lauren, and decided that he wanted to get to know Lauren better! She glowed with happiness.

'Is this . . . for me?' she asked, rereading the words on the paper.

Marcus nodded and smiled. 'I thought you could pass it on to your friend Jennifer, if you wouldn't mind. I tried to give it to her last night, but she had to rush off and didn't come back online. But you could give it to her, couldn't you? Seeing as she's your best friend and everything.'

Lauren suddenly felt sick. She nodded mutely, trying not to show the disappointment she felt.

'Thanks, Lauren – that's brilliant! I knew I could count on you. How soon can you give it to her?' Marcus said, beaming.

Well – at least he got my name right, Lauren thought. She pulled herself together. 'Tonight,' she replied, raising the best smile that she could. 'I'll give it to Jennifer tonight.'

After supper, Lauren sat at her PC, head in hands. She didn't know what to do. All she had ever wanted was to get close to Marcus and fit in. But her plan was backfiring because all *he* wanted was to talk to Jennifer. She looked miserably at the scrap of paper on her desk.

She weighed things up. If she gave it all up now, she would go back into obscurity. Lauren shuddered at the thought of it. But if she kept up the lie and carried on pretending to be Jennifer, then she could continue putting in a good word for herself. Eventually, Marcus might come to see her in a new light and realize he preferred her to Jennifer. The whole thing could actually work out in her favour.

Feeling more positive, Lauren wasted no time in creating a brand new email address for Jennifer to use.

'Perfect,' she said to herself.

Lauren saved Marcus's email address in Jennifer's address book, and then she began to compose an email to him from Jennifer.

Hi Marcus,

Got your address from Lauren today. Heard you want to chat off the forum. Sounds good to me.

Jen.

After the briefest time, there was 'one new message' in Jennifer's inbox. Lauren smiled. Marcus must have been waiting for her to email.

Hi Jen,

That's right. Glad Lauren did what I asked her. What r u up to tonight? R u doing homework or something more interesting?

Marcus.

Lauren thought for a moment and then hit the 'reply' button.

Me and Lauren r having a sleepover. I doubt I'll get any sleep at all tonight because she is such a good laugh we'll probably still be giggling when the sun comes up tomorrow!
Jx

Lauren emailed Marcus all evening, pretending to be Jennifer and taking every opportunity to write herself up in his eyes. It was midnight when she eventually logged off. Feeling exhilarated, she flopped down into her bed, but then a thought entered her head – she hadn't done her homework! It was due to be handed in first period tomorrow, and normally the very thought of getting into trouble with a teacher would have terrified her. But for some reason it didn't. Tonight, Lauren could only think about her correspondence with Marcus, until tiredness eventually claimed her and she fell asleep.

Mr Price's maths lesson came round all too soon for Lauren. She arrived for class five minutes late with dark, puffy eyes from lack of sleep.

'So, Lauren. You've decided to grace us with your presence, have you?' said Mr Price. 'I trust you come bearing your algebra homework.'

She hadn't, and now she hated the thought of being in trouble. She could feel herself shrinking in front of the teacher and her classmates. But then something in her made her stop. *What would Jennifer do?* she asked herself. Lauren noticed Marcus smiling at her from the back of the classroom, and in that moment, she found exactly the right words to say. 'I slept over at a friend's house last night, sir, and I'm afraid I left my maths homework there. I only remembered at the bus stop but when I went back to fetch it, her parents had already left for work so I couldn't get in. By that time the bus had gone. That's why I'm late.'

To Lauren's amazement, Mr Price waved her away with a hand, saying, 'Next time, don't be so careless. I'll expect it in tomorrow. No excuses.'

'Yes, sir,' Lauren replied, and made her way to her

desk. Even though she was tired, she suddenly felt fantastic! *Anyone who says that lying doesn't pay obviously isn't a good liar himself*, she thought, smiling.

She was still smiling about how well she'd managed to avoid trouble when she arrived at the school canteen. The place was packed, and it looked as if Lauren was out of luck for anywhere to sit. But just then, she noticed Angie Johnson, one of the coolest girls in the school, get up from her seat and motion towards her.

Lauren turned around, thinking Angie must be waving at someone standing behind her. But there was nobody else there.

'Hey, Lauren,' called Angie. 'There's a seat over here.'

Lauren walked over and sat down next to Angie. 'Hi,' she said.

'You're a friend of Jennifer's, aren't you?' Angie began. 'Well, I'm having a party at the weekend and I thought you guys might like to come. I've chatted with her on The Outer Zone and she seems pretty cool.'

Lauren couldn't believe it. It was her first party invite, and to top it off, it was from Angie Johnson! She composed herself. 'That sounds great, Angie – let me speak to Jennifer and I'll get back to you.'

Lauren dimly remembered chatting with someone named AnnG. She thought back to their discussion about modelling. She'd had no idea she'd been giving style advice to a girl as cool as Angie.

Chantelle arrived at their table. 'I see you've got an unwanted guest here, Angie,' she said curtly.

'Do you mean Lauren?' Angie replied. 'She's not unwanted. In fact, I was just inviting her and Jennifer to my party this weekend.'

Lauren watched as Chantelle's face started to resemble a chewed toffee. She suppressed a giggle.

'That's right,' Lauren added, looking Chantelle directly in the eye, 'and I think *we* can come, providing Jennifer hasn't got a modelling job or anything.'

Wordlessly, Chantelle sat down and stared at her lunch. Angie sat down next to Lauren. 'Sorry about that,' she began. 'Now, tell me about Jen! It must be great having a model for a friend. You must get to share her clothes and everything.'

'Oh, yes,' replied Lauren. 'Jen's dead generous. Last week she gave me a pair of brand new sandals. But then again, she's always been like that – ever since we met that first term in primary school.'

'Wait a second,' interrupted Chantelle. 'Marcus told me that you two met at some sort of hospital charity dinner. Which one is it, Lauren? The dinner, or school?'

Lauren swallowed hard. *Was that really what she had told Marcus? That they had met at a charity do?* She thought back. It was true, she remembered telling him. Angie looked uncertain, her pretty features creased into a frown. Inside, Lauren kicked herself for making such a stupid mistake.

'Er . . . that's right, we did,' she said slowly, thinking on her feet, 'and coincidentally, we both started at the same school the next day! That's why I got things muddled up. It was a while ago, after all.'

To Lauren's relief, the lie seemed to have the desired effect: Chantelle didn't challenge her any more, and Angie seemed fine again. But it highlighted a problem. Lauren was beginning to tell so many lies about Jennifer, she was having difficulty remembering exactly what she'd said to whom. As she threw away her leftovers, she realized that she'd have to think of a way to fix the problem.

During her next study period, Lauren wrote everything down so that she wouldn't forget what she had said about Jennifer: her height, eye colour, hair colour, likes, dislikes, friends, family and hobbies. She put it all in a card folder and tucked the file into her schoolbag. Once it was finished, Lauren smiled. There was no way she could be caught out now.

That evening, Marcus was at football practice, so Lauren decided not to bother going on The Outer

Zone. She contented herself by listening to music and reading the new magazines she had bought on the way home from school.

But even though it had been another good day, Lauren slept badly. She had a vivid dream about Jennifer. She was walking into Angie's party, and everyone was there – including Marcus. Soon, she was making her way through the crowd, and everyone was smiling and saying hello to her. And then she found herself dancing next to a blonde girl who looked like the model out of her magazine. *It's Jennifer*, she realized in a jolt. But this Jennifer certainly didn't seem to be the good friend that Lauren had created. *This* Jennifer turned around and stared her up and down, and Lauren could feel a wall of self-consciousness closing up around her. And then this Jennifer began to laugh, and kept laughing at her; the sound grated on Lauren's ears.

'Please, stop it!' Lauren said, trying to eye a way out, but failing because the party was so full. She could see Marcus nearby, but he was ignoring her, and seemed to be staring at Jennifer.

Then Jennifer began taunting her. 'You'll get caught . . .' she said mockingly. 'You know it can't last.'

Lauren tried desperately to dance away from Jennifer, but Angie's party was packed, and she couldn't get through the crowd. Suddenly, Jennifer lunged out and grabbed Lauren's arm so tightly she could feel nails sinking into her skin. Lauren shouted at her to stop. But Jennifer seemed to find this funny, throwing back her head and laughing whilst the grip on Lauren's arm grew tighter and tighter.

She awoke with a jolt and turned on the bedside lamp. The dream was so real and terrifying, she felt she needed to look at her wrist. But there was no mark. Nothing. Lauren's heart still thumped in her chest. She looked at the alarm clock – it said 3:12. Leaving the light on, Lauren rolled over and tried not to think about Jennifer.

* * *

Lauren arrived at the school gate tired and flustered. The late nights were starting to tell on her now. Last night's bad dream hadn't helped much either and Lauren was still trying to shake it off when she got to class. By lunchtime, her head was throbbing. She was beginning to feel tetchy; all anybody seemed to want to talk to her about was Jennifer.

'Will Jennifer be modelling at London Fashion Week?' asked Angie.

Or, from the boys: 'Has Jennifer got a date for Angie's party?'

Even though it had been Lauren who had created Jennifer, she was starting to get tired of the whole thing. She almost wished herself anonymous again so she could get a bit of peace and quiet.

As she walked out towards the playground, she heard footsteps from behind her. It was Josie, Chantelle's friend who'd been mean to her when she first posted on the website.

'Hi, Lauren,' said Josie, 'I've been looking for you everywhere! Anyway, I wanted to tell you that I met your friend Jennifer in town on Saturday. Isn't that great?'

Lauren felt as though her heart had stopped. 'Are you sure?' she replied.

'Oh yeah,' continued Josie. 'I was buying some new jeans when I noticed her standing at the till. Of course, I knew it was Jennifer straight away, long blonde hair, size eight figure and those legs . . . well, no wonder she's a model!'

Lauren tried to see whether Josie had been somehow put up to this. Was she trying to trick her? Josie appeared to be telling the truth. *But it didn't make sense*. There was no way she could have met Jennifer, because Jennifer didn't exist.

'Did you speak to her?' Lauren asked, recovering enough to think a little more clearly. 'Did she actually tell you who she was?'

Josie nodded. 'Oh yes. I asked her name and she told me she was called Jennifer. She was dead nice about it.'

'And what happened then?'

'Well,' Josie continued, 'it was her turn to be served, so we didn't really have any time to chat. By the time I was finished, she was gone. Probably due at another modelling job or something . . .'

That night, Lauren checked her emails before dinner. She was now amused by her encounter with Josie. For a minute, Lauren had been really worried, until she'd reminded herself that Jennifer was imaginary, and only existed because Lauren allowed her to. Lauren had reached the conclusion that Josie had seen a pretty girl who fitted Jennifer's description, and simply assumed it was her. The fact that she was also called Jennifer was a coincidence and nothing more.

Lauren's inbox indicated that she had mail and Lauren clicked it open, wondering if it was Marcus. But the name of the sender suddenly sent her blood cold.

It was from Jennifer.

With fingers shaking, Lauren opened the message.

Hiya,

Spoke to Marcus, he's luvvly. Can't wait 2 meet him. Can u fix it up?

Jxxxxxxxxxxx

Lauren felt sick. What on earth was going on? There was no way Jennifer could have sent Lauren an email. She wasn't even real! Lauren tried to keep calm, but her hands were shaking so much that she couldn't control the mouse. Thought upon thought crashed into her mind. *If Jennifer hadn't sent it, then who had? It might be someone who suspected what Lauren was up to. They might have hacked into the email account and be trying to catch her out.*

With a hurried click, she deleted the message. If Lauren replied, she was sure that she'd fall into a trap – whoever it was would have her.

'Lauren, dinner!' her mother shouted, and with some relief, Lauren closed down her PC.

'Coming!' she called. As she turned the light off in her room, Lauren thought hard about who could have sent the email from Jennifer. The person right at the top of her list was Chantelle Dawson.

Lauren ate her dinner in silence. Her stomach was churning so hard that she could hardly eat a mouthful. The late nights and talk of Jennifer had made her tired, confused and edgy. She excused herself from the table and made for her bed.

But as soon as sleep came, so did a nightmare. And this one was worse than the last. Lauren was at Angie's party, and she was walking through the crowds, but now, instead of everyone dancing, they stood staring at her. The music around them blared, but they were all silent as the grave. Soon, a sickly sweet fragrance came wafting into Lauren's nostrils. She could feel herself gag, but as she looked for a window to get some fresh air, she saw Jennifer striding up to her. The smell was Jennifer's perfume, and it was overpowering.

'Hi, Lauren – welcome back,' she said with a sneer

running across her carefully made up face. And with that, the party exploded into life, but everyone began to dance at a crazy, breakneck pace that made Lauren feel sicker and dizzier.

'I have to get out – I'm choking,' she said to Jennifer, but her words were drowned out by the heavy, thumping music. Lauren felt her throat tighten. 'I can't breathe! Please help me!' she pleaded, but no one was listening. She saw Marcus nearby, and she ran to him, clutching at his arm. He looked at her without any recognition and shrugged away from her roughly. 'Let me out!' she heard herself scream. Jennifer watched from nearby, dancing to the beat, laughing at Lauren.

'You're going to get caught!' she laughed. 'Your time is nearly up!'

Lauren desperately struggled to get out. She pushed against the wall of people as hard as she could. She had to get out of this place – away from Jennifer. But the throng held solid, and suddenly she felt the pressure of Jennifer's hand around her arm, and the nails sink into her skin. This time it was much more painful.

'Stop it!' she screamed. 'Go away! You're not real!'

'I'm part of you now,' Jennifer said, gripping her arm even tighter. 'I'm *never* going away.'

'Jen!

'Jen!'

Lauren woke in a cold sweat. The duvet was on the floor and her hair was soaked to her forehead. Her mum was standing over her.

'You were screaming in your sleep, love – are you all right?' her mum said, an anxious look on her face.

'I'm . . . fine, Mum, thanks,' Lauren muttered. Her mum gave her a hug, and turned to leave.

'Mum . . . what did you call me just then?' Lauren asked. But her mum had gone.

Lauren's door was open a crack, and a sliver of light from the hallway shone in. Her eyes fell upon her arm, and there, unmistakably, was a red hand mark.

Terrified, she got out of bed and hurried to the

bathroom. Under the harsh fluorescent glare, she examined her wrist, turning it over underneath the cold water. There were five red marks on her arm – four in a row and one on the underside. Her skin tingled and burned as the water ran over the bruises. *Could I have done this to myself in my sleep?* Lauren thought. As she made her way back to bed, she couldn't help but feel that things were beginning to slip out of her control.

Lauren decided not to go to Angie's party – it was far easier than having to come up with a reason why Jennifer couldn't come. Her dream had really scared her, and Lauren hoped that school might take her mind off everything.

Over the weekend, she thought a lot about the strange email from Jennifer, and the more Lauren thought about it, the more she was sure that it must have come from Chantelle. From the very start, it had always been she who'd doubted Lauren's lies.

Lauren waited in the cold for the bus on Monday morning. There were a large group of her classmates nearby, jumping up and down on the spot to keep warm and chatting about their weekend, but Lauren wasn't in the mood to get involved. As the bus arrived, she stood at the front of the queue, desperate to get out of the cold. Chantelle and her friends sat at the back of the bus as usual and Lauren steeled herself for a barrage of questions about Jennifer.

'All right,' she nodded at them, trying to look casual.

'All right,' Chantelle and Josie nodded back. 'Did you hear from Jennifer this weekend, then?'

Lauren stopped, waiting for the sting in the tail of the question. But that's all they said. Lauren chose her words carefully. 'Jennifer was busy. So no, I didn't see her,' she replied, dumping her schoolbag on the seat next to her.

Josie merely looked disappointed, whilst Chantelle just gave a shrug. There were no comments about emails, no sarcastic remarks. Nothing.

Lauren slid quietly into her seat and leaned her head against the window and closed her eyes. Perhaps she had been too quick in suspecting Chantelle after all.

Even Marcus sitting down next to her failed to make her feel better about things. 'Hey, Lauren,' he said. 'I just want to thank you for introducing me to Jennifer. She's such a great girl.'

'You've already said,' replied Lauren curtly.

'Well, it's true! I can't stop thinking about her – especially after last night.'

'Last night?' The comment made Lauren sit up and look at him. 'What about last night?'

'We were talking on Instant Messenger all night. Honestly, Lauren, that girl is so funny and cool, I can't wait to meet her.'

'Are you sure?' Lauren asked, staring at him hard. 'I mean, are you sure it was last night?'

Marcus frowned. 'Of course I'm sure.'

Lauren sat back, feeling numb. *This can't be happening*, she thought. *I wasn't online all weekend*. Lauren began to feel her head spin. She touched her bruised arm, and felt tears coming to her eyes. *I wish I'd never started the whole thing*.

As soon as they arrived at the school gates, Lauren grabbed her bag, pushed past Marcus and ran to the girls' bathroom. She had an overwhelming feeling that she was going to be sick. She frantically rooted round inside her bag. It was high time she ended the Jennifer thing; it was becoming a complete nightmare. The Jennifer file would be the first thing to go. She would rip it into shreds and flush it down the toilet. Lauren pulled the folder from her bag and opened it.

It was empty.

She gasped in horror and turned her bag inside out. At the bottom of her bag, a crunched up piece of paper hit the toilet floor. She picked it up and opened it.

Hi, Lauren,

Looking for your notes? If you want them back then you'd better meet me lunchtime in the art block.

Chantelle

The minutes inched by like hours and finally it was lunchtime. Lauren headed for the art block. Chantelle was ready and waiting for her when she arrived. To Lauren's absolute dismay, she had brought a crowd with her, including Marcus.

'Well, here she is,' Chantelle announced with a smirk. 'And I think you're all going to enjoy hearing what Lauren's got to tell us!'

'What are you playing at, Chantelle?' demanded Marcus. 'I thought you said we were here about Jennifer.'

'And so we are,' Chantelle said, staring hard at Lauren. 'Lauren here is going to tell us all about *Jennifer*, aren't you?'

Lauren was terrified. From the smug look on Chantelle's face, she was sure all her lies about

Jennifer were about to be exposed. Lauren would be a complete social outcast. Frantically she tried to think of something plausible to say, but her mind went blank.

'Nothing to say?' said Chantelle, walking towards her. 'How about I tell everyone what a liar you are.' She turned to face everyone. 'Lauren's famous friend Jennifer doesn't *exist.*'

There was a moment's silence and then everyone began to talk amongst themselves. Lauren's face burned with shame.

'It's not true, is it, Lauren?' demanded Marcus. She could see in his eyes that he was hoping desperately Chantelle was wrong.

Lauren's mouth moved silently as she tried and failed to answer.

'Of course it's true,' said Chantelle. 'And here's the proof.' Out of her bag, Chantelle extracted the notes about Jennifer that Lauren had written. Lauren could feel the blood draining from her face, and she felt dizzy. This was the worst thing that could have happened: she knew that the proof of all her lies was right there in front of her classmates – in Lauren's own handwriting. There was no way she could deny it.

'Excuse me – what's going on?' A voice interrupted the crowd. It sounded familiar to Lauren, but she couldn't place it. The group opened up to reveal an impossibly beautiful girl with tumbling blonde curls and legs like a racehorse. 'Oh *there* you are, Lauren!' she said. 'I've been looking everywhere for you.'

The crowd peeled away and let the girl through. She flashed her pretty blue eyes at Marcus.

'You must be Marcus,' she said, touching his fingers a tad too long. 'You look just like you sound online.'

Marcus stammered incoherently at her.

'Jennifer?' Lauren asked in an incredulous whisper.

The blonde whirled round to face Lauren. 'Of course! Who else did you think it was? Now where's my file you were looking after?'

Jennifer took the papers back from Chantelle,

whose cheeks were beetroot red. 'Well, I'm so relieved you had my file, Lauren. I've been looking everywhere for it.' She gave a nod to Chantelle and the others. Their faces were a picture of astonishment. 'Sorry to dash but nice to meet you all at last.' Jennifer touched Lauren on the arm, and she felt warm to touch. Then Lauren smelled something which made her head spin and her throat tighten; it was sickly sweet and flowery. It was the smell of the perfume from Lauren's nightmare.

'I've got to talk to you,' Lauren demanded as she went after Jennifer.

Jennifer stopped immediately and beamed. 'Of course. What is it you want?'

Lauren looked the girl squarely in the face and hesitated. She knew what she was about to say might sound really, really stupid. 'You're not Jennifer,' she said. 'So who *are* you?'

The girl gave her a puzzled look. 'What are you talking about, Lauren? Of course I'm Jennifer.' She motioned to the file. 'I was at your house last night, for heaven's sake. You were helping me with my autobiography project for Social Studies. When I couldn't find it this morning, I figured I must have left it in your rucksack. So I just popped in to collect it. I didn't think you'd be upset about it.'

Lauren's head was spinning. This couldn't be happening. It was impossible. She tried to protest. 'But . . . but you're not even . . . real,' she said. 'I made you up! You *can't* be here. You can't be Jennifer!' But she knew that what she was saying sounded ridiculous – especially when the proof was standing in front of her.

She swayed dangerously and Jennifer only just managed to stop her from falling to the floor. 'Crikey, Lauren! Stop acting so weird! We've known each other for years.' She helped Lauren steady herself before giving her a concerned smile. 'You really ought to get an early night tonight, you know.'

The girl began to head towards the front gate and

Lauren shouted to her. 'Where are you going?' she asked.

'Back to school, of course! But I'll see you tonight, Lauren, just like we planned.'

And with that, she was gone. Lauren watched her walk through the gates and down the street, her blonde hair swinging down her back like a snake.

The sensible part of Lauren's brain told her there was no way the girl could have been Jennifer. It was impossible, surely. Everything was beginning to blur, and she was finding it really hard to distinguish between truth and reality. Lauren genuinely wondered if she was going mad. If only she had someone to confide in about this whole thing. Someone impartial and understanding.

Lauren found it hard to talk to Mrs Williams at first because she'd never sought help from a school counsellor before. But, after a faltering start, everything came tumbling out: Lauren's tall stories and all the deceit. It was a tremendous relief to finally get the whole sorry affair out into the open.

By the time she'd finished, tears were streaming down Lauren's face. '. . . And now Jennifer's turned up here. But you see, she *can't* have because she's not even real.' Lauren choked back a sob. 'Oh, please help me. The whole thing's sending me crazy.'

Mrs Williams didn't make a murmur. Instead she looked thoughtful. 'Now, Lauren,' she said slowly, 'you wouldn't be talking about Jennifer Tynan, would you? I've known Jennifer since she was a little girl. Comes from a lovely family, too.'

Lauren's eyes widened in astonishment. 'You *know* Jennifer?' she said, staring at the counsellor in disbelief.

'Of course,' nodded Mrs Williams. '*Everyone* knows Jennifer. She does a bit of modelling, I believe. Very pretty girl.'

'I . . . have to go,' Lauren said, and left the office. Tears fell from her face. She didn't have a clue what was going on, but she had come to one definite conclusion: nobody wanted to listen to anything rational she had to say on the subject of Jennifer. Lauren was on her own.

She made her way towards class, wiping her face and trying to pull herself together. 'I'll go along with things for the time being,' she whispered to herself, 'but if she turns up again, I'm going to get right to the bottom of this.'

Lauren didn't have to wait too long. As she rounded the corner of the Resources block, she saw a tall, blonde girl waiting outside the headmaster's office.

'Jennifer?' she gasped.

Jennifer beamed at her.

'I . . . I thought you'd gone back to your school?' Lauren managed.

Jennifer blushed. 'Well, I couldn't tell you the truth, could I? After all, I had to keep things secret until I was a hundred per cent sure.'

'Sure about what?'

'Well,' replied Jennifer with a giggle, 'I've just been to see the headmaster and had my final interview to switch schools. I'm starting here this afternoon. Now we'll *always* be together, Lauren. Isn't it great?'

Lauren began to back away.

'Where are you going, Lauren?' Jennifer asked, still smiling at her.

'Away from here and away from you!' Lauren screamed, turning to run. But Jennifer was too fast for her.

'Calm down there, friend,' she said, grabbing Lauren by the arm. Lauren could feel Jennifer's powerful grip, smell her sickening perfume all around. Suddenly, she was fighting for breath, and she felt weak.

'But . . . you're not real,' Lauren said, defeated.

She recognized the look in Jennifer's eyes as she turned to face her. Lauren had seen it before in her nightmare.

'Don't be silly,' Jennifer said in a flat, terrifying voice. 'I'm more real than you are!'

The rest of the afternoon passed in a blur, and the next thing Lauren knew she was on the bus home.

She was sitting at the front of the bus again, a from the gossip. Her head felt far too fragile to able to handle it.

It was a massive relief when Lauren finally reache her front door. She looked up and down, and everything seemed normal. For the first time in weeks, Lauren felt like reading some textbooks and doing some homework. She turned the key in the lock.

'Mum! Dad!' she called. *They must be working late*, she thought, as she made her way to the kitchen to make a snack. But as she entered the kitchen, a tall, willowy figure came out of the lounge and stood in front of her.

'What are you doing in my house?' Jennifer asked.

Lauren stared at her in horror. 'I'm ignoring you,' she shouted, throwing her schoolbag on the floor. 'I don't know what you're trying to do but this is *my* house and you are *not* real!'

Jennifer didn't move. Instead she folded her arms and smiled in amusement.

It was the smile that Lauren remembered from her

lt her throat tighten as she backed ifer. 'You're not real,' she said again. o thought you up! You're just a figment gination.'

nnifer stepped in front of her, blocking the ll. She was still smiling. Lauren closed her , and she could smell Jennifer's hot, sweet rfume close to her.

'I think you'll find it's the other way round, Lauren,' Jennifer whispered. *'You're* a figment of *my* imagination.'

Lauren's heart thundered so hard against her chest she thought she would faint. She pushed past Jennifer. *I have to get out of here,* Lauren thought frantically. *I have to find my parents and tell them what's going on.* Just then, Lauren heard the key in the front door, and a wave of relief washed over her – her father was back from work.

'Dad, thank goodness you're home! I've been so—' Lauren stopped, mid-sentence. Her dad wasn't looking at her.

He seemed to be looking *through* her.

Lauren's father walked over to Jennifer and gave her a big hug. 'Jennifer, sweetheart,' Lauren heard him say, 'were you talking to yourself again? We've discussed this, haven't we? You're too old to have an imaginary friend.'

'You're right, Dad,' Jennifer replied. Lauren looked on, mute with terror and confusion. 'But don't worry. I'm pretty sure she's gone now . . . for ever.'

TICKETS PLEASE

As Brian Magee chipped the dented Coke can with his foot, he could almost hear the roar of the crowd in his ears. The can rattled obligingly along the narrow lane bordering the railway sidings, bouncing off the rusty iron fence, landing smack bang in front of his best friend Craig's waiting foot.

'Great pass, Magee!' grinned Craig, dribbling the tin noisily along the tarmac.

Out of nowhere, a thin, wiry girl wearing a green

and yellow striped football shirt darted in front of him and deftly wrestled the can away with a flick of her foot. Brian groaned as he watched her take it right down the lane towards the railway station, the number seven on her shirt getting smaller and smaller.

'What did you let her do that for?' Brian complained. 'We almost scored.'

'This is *Emily* you're talking about,' Craig replied. 'If she wasn't a girl, she'd be the best striker in the whole school. You try tackling her!'

'I heard that,' shouted Emily from the end of the lane. 'But it's got nothing to do with me being a girl, Craig. You couldn't tackle a paper bag!'

Brian laughed and tied a green and yellow scarf around both wrists. He was well aware of Emily's skill as a footballer. It was one of the reasons they were such good mates. That and their undying devotion for their town's favourite football team. 'Yeah, well, *I'm* going to be the best striker and if I was playing this afternoon, we'd definitely hammer this Rovers side.'

Craig nodded keenly. 'And the cup would be ours to bring home.'

'I can't wait to get to the game, can you?' said Brian. 'Seven years since our team last took the cup! They're definitely going to win it today, though. That new striker's a dead cert to score.'

'Yeah,' agreed Craig. 'It's just a shame they couldn't play here at home.'

Brian shrugged. 'Home or away, it makes no difference! History is about to be made.'

Emily shouted for them to hurry up. 'Come on, you two. If we miss this train we miss the match and there's no way we'd be able to walk to the stadium in time!'

Brian broke into a run. 'She's right. We'd better get a move on. We don't want the train to leave without us.'

They roared with excitement and sped down the lane towards the ancient brick building that served as the railway office.

Today it stood quietly in the summer sunshine,

eaves dripping with bright hanging baskets. Emily waited outside, flopped on a wooden bench, her cheeks red with exertion. The can lay at her feet.

Brian immediately scooped it up with a toe and began playing keepie-uppie.

Emily rummaged in her pockets. 'Craig, have you got the cash for the train?'

'I thought you were bringing it!' Craig was looking defensive.

Brian groaned. 'I don't believe it! Craig, we *needed* that money! You said you were going to borrow it from your mum!'

'Sorry, guys,' Craig said quietly. 'I just totally forgot.'

'*Now* what are we going to do?' Emily said, exasperated. 'Brian – how much cash have you got on you?'

Brian considered the change in his pocket. 'Umm, along with my ticket for the game, I've got about a pound left over.'

'I've got about the same,' Craig said glumly.

'Me too,' Emily sighed. 'So not one of us has enough for a train ticket. We don't even have time to go all the way back into town to get some cash out. What are we going to do? We can't miss the match!'

Brian was serious for a moment. 'I've got an idea,' he said, suddenly. 'Why don't we just skip the train fare?'

Emily shook her head. 'But that's against the law. I mean, what if we get caught?'

'We won't. Blackwell's only a couple of stops.'

Emily wasn't convinced. 'But what if an inspector gets on and asks to see our tickets?'

Brian thought for a moment. 'It's not very likely is it, Em? I mean, whenever we've been to away matches before, we've never been asked to show our tickets. The train's always too crowded.'

Craig grinned. 'Brian's right. I've never even seen a ticket inspector on the train.'

Emily looked doubtful. 'And what will we use to bail us out of prison when we're caught?'

'Oh, don't be so melodramatic, Em!' said Craig. 'You're always looking at the negative bits.'

'Well, it's just as well I do. You're such an idiot you never see the downside in any of Brian's plans. That's why you're both always in detention!'

Brian, sensing a row, plonked himself between them on the bench. 'Calm down, you two. It's too hot to fight. And besides, it's not as though we'll end up like my Great-uncle Ray.'

'I didn't know you had a Great-uncle Ray,' said Emily. 'You've never mentioned him.'

Brian shook his head. 'That's the point. *Nobody* in the family mentions him. It brings back bad memories.'

Craig's eyes widened. 'Why, what happened?'

'Well,' said Brian. 'It's a bit of a mystery, really. Great-uncle Ray was a fan like us and never missed a match. Apparently, the whole thing happened when he was thirteen—'

'That's our age,' said Craig.

'Doing better in maths, huh, Craig?' Emily said, laughing.

'Anyway,' Brian interrupted loudly, 'according to my Aunt Josie, Great-uncle Ray took a train from this station and was never seen again!'

'Rubbish,' laughed Emily. 'How could he just disappear into thin air?'

'It's true,' said Brian, his face deadly serious. 'When the train arrived at its destination, his football rattle and scarf were arranged neatly on a seat but he was nowhere to be found. And no one ever saw him again.'

There was silence for a moment before Craig shook his head. 'Wow, that's spooky.'

'I might have known *you'd* believe him, Craig,' groaned Emily.

Brian got to his feet. He knew that the trains from this station were always at least ten minutes late but he didn't want to take any chances. They were going to be on the train whatever happened.

'Look, I'm going to risk not buying a ticket. Come on – it's only once . . . Who's with me?'

Craig was immediately at Brian's side, grinning. 'I am.'

Brian looked pleadingly at Emily. 'Oh, come on. It won't be the same without you.'

She rolled her eyes and grinned. 'OK, I still think you're being an idiot but if you're not paying, then neither am I.'

Brian looked at his watch. Their train was due in five minutes, but considering the team was playing a cup match, the station was deserted. In fact, apart from them, it was completely empty.

'It's a bit quiet today,' wondered Craig.

'Perhaps most of the other fans have taken an earlier train,' suggested Emily. 'After all, kick-off's at two.'

But Brian had noticed another person on the platform. The ticket seller was ensconced inside his little wooden booth, reading the newspaper.

'What about him?' he whispered to the others. 'We can't risk him seeing us.'

Emily drew them into a huddle. 'I've thought of that,' she said. 'We'll creep past him and hide in the waiting-room until the train arrives. Then, when the whistle goes, we'll dash out, and run on the train as it pulls out.'

Brian was impressed. 'I thought you weren't keen on the idea, Em. Now you're acting like a Great Train Robber!' he joked.

Emily put her hands on her hips. 'Are you complaining?'

Brian laughed. 'No, no. It's a great idea! Come on, let's go.'

They pressed themselves against the station wall and crept, one by one, towards the waiting-room door. As they passed the tiny wooden booth, Brian saw that the ticket seller had his back to them. His feet were up, a newspaper spread out on his lap, and nearby, steam swirled from a mug of tea.

'That's a good job,' whispered Craig. 'Drinking tea and listening to the radio. My dad would love that.'

An old-fashioned band tune drifted through the small round ticket hole in the glass window. Brian stifled a laugh. 'Don't think much of his taste in music, though.'

'No,' agreed Emily. 'It's almost as bad as yours!' She stifled a giggle.

Despite their laughter, Brian couldn't help feeling a slight prickle of apprehension. Emily and Craig darted inside the safe walls of the waiting-room but Brian lingered for a moment. Despite the fact the ticket seller still had his back to him, he couldn't help feeling the guy was somehow watching him. And there was something about the ticket seller's hair. Nestling amongst the man's thatch of jet was a bright, almost white streak. It made him look just like a badger. Brian had never seen anything like it before.

'What are you doing out there?' he heard Emily hiss.

Brian tore himself away and dashed for the door.

The waiting-room lay to one side of the platform, a little way up from the ticket seller's small wooden booth and, thankfully, out of his line of sight.

'How much longer is the train going to be?' moaned Craig.

He and Emily settled down to wait on one of the hard wooden benches. Brian passed the time studying the announcements on the waiting-room notice-board. There was an old yellowing timetable held up by a single rusted drawing pin, a dog-eared advert which looked as if it had been there for at least fifty years and a large notice with a rip down the centre. It read:

Failure to travel with a valid ticket will result in

The rest of the poster was missing. Brian was just wondering what it might have said, when he heard the unmistakable sound of a train's brakes.

'At last,' said Craig, jumping up.

A surge of excitement rushed through Brian's body as he checked the waiting-room window. Another minute or so and they would all be safely on the train.

'It's not a regular train,' he reported to the others.

'What do you mean?' asked Craig.

'I mean it's one of those old-fashioned ones with the locking doors. I thought they went out of service years ago.'

Emily pushed her way beside him. 'No, they still use them sometimes when the others are being serviced.'

A whistle sounded, and it looked as though the train was going to depart. Brian took a deep breath and darted through the waiting-room door. 'Come on!' he yelled to Emily and Craig. 'Let's go!'

They broke into a run. Brian took the lead and, as they reached the ticket booth, his eyes searched for the ticket seller. Thankfully, he was still inside the booth, hidden behind his newspaper. Brian upped his pace. By the time the old geezer realized what they were up to it would be miles too late to stop them.

Suddenly, from the corner of his eye, Brian saw the ticket seller rise up in his chair and bang furiously on the glass with his fist.

'Don't you dare get on that train without a ticket!' he roared.

Brian's chest began to pound. The others were right behind him, but were any of them close enough to make it?

Brian could still hear the ticket seller shouting behind him. 'Stop!' he was yelling. 'Come back here!'

But it was too late to stop now, and Brian ignored him, pelting at top speed towards the nearest carriage door and grabbing the handle. To his surprise, it refused to budge.

'Hurry up!' yelled Emily, close on his heels.

'Come on, you stupid thing!' Brian shouted at the door. 'Open!' He tugged and pulled furiously at the brass handle but it remained steadfastly shut. 'I can't budge it,' he said, abandoning his efforts. 'I'll try the next one down.'

It was a long sprint down the platform and Brian found himself running alongside a carriage packed with passengers. Despite the panic, he couldn't mistake the blur of yellow and green football shirts pressed against the window. The train began to creak and groan as it moved away from the station.

We're going to win the cup today, Brian thought, *and I'm going to be there to see it!* He reached for the handle on the next carriage. The ticket seller's shouts were louder now, more urgent.

'You'll be sorry!' he yelled. 'Don't say I didn't warn you!'

'Quick – open it,' yelled Craig, hot on his heels.

Brian gave the handle a yank and the door creaked open. The three of them leaped on board and slammed the door firmly behind them, just as the train began to pick up speed.

'How cool was that!' whooped Brian.

'That was brilliant,' agreed Emily, trying desperately to catch her breath.

Craig held on to his knees, panting. 'It was better than brilliant. It was awesome!'

The three of them flopped thankfully down into nearby seats, cheeks red from the chase. Brian took the opportunity to gaze around, noticing how different the set-up of the train carriage was to that of a modern train. There were open areas, which he was sure were for normal travellers, and old-fashioned compartments with sliding doors.

'I've just had a terrible thought,' Emily said. 'We *are* on the right train, aren't we?'

The grin left Brian's face. In all the excitement he hadn't thought to check. 'This has to be the right train. I noticed a carriage full of supporters.'

'Did you hear that ticket seller shouting at us?' giggled Emily. 'I thought he was going to blow a gasket he was so angry.'

'I know,' agreed Brian. 'It was a close one.'

'The door handle was a bit of a heart stopper, though,' said Emily, feeling the mock leather seats with her hand. 'These old trains are really strange, aren't they? Even the seats are weird.' She shifted about uncomfortably. 'I'm glad we're only going a few stops.'

Brian explored the small compartment they were

in. 'It reminds me of an old black and white film I saw once. Everyone was sitting in a cubicle just like this when the train went through a tunnel. Anyway, when they came out of the other side one of the passengers was missing. All that was left was an empty seat. Dead creepy it was. They spent the rest of the film looking for the body.'

Craig stood on his seat and reached inside the large shelf above their heads. 'Did they find it up here?' he asked.

Brian got up beside him. 'No, that's for luggage.'

Craig grinned. 'I *know*. My dad used to travel to work every day on a train like this. He talks about it quite a lot, especially when he's late home. He reckons these old models were far more reliable than the newer ones.'

'You don't get these compartments on modern trains, either,' said Emily, sliding open a glass door beside them. 'I think it's nicer. A bit like travelling in your own little room.'

They peered out. A central corridor ran the full

length of the carriage ahead. Craig got up and went off to investigate.

'Should he be doing that?' Emily asked. 'I mean, haven't we taken enough risks already? We don't want to get caught now.'

'Relax, Em,' Brian said, trying his best to reassure her. 'I'm sure it'll be fine.'

Craig called out excitedly from the other end of the carriage. 'Hey, guys, feast your eyes on this! It's a first class compartment. Fancy travelling in a bit of style?'

'Yeah!' cried Brian, heading eagerly along the corridor. He'd hardly made it through the door before Emily caught him by the arm.

'Look,' she said seriously. 'There could be a guard on board.'

They heard Craig's voice boom impatiently from the end of the corridor. 'Did you see how empty the station was?' He rolled his eyes in exasperation. 'If there are no passengers, then *of course* there won't be any guards. Why don't you both just relax!'

To Brian's relief, Emily managed a smile. 'You're probably right,' she said. 'Anyway, I expect our team always travels first class!'

'Too right,' said Brian, giving her a gentle shove down the aisle.

'You two need to chill,' advised Craig, waiting for them at the door. 'I mean, can you see any guards on this train?'

Brian and Emily shook their heads.

'Exactly. There aren't even any other passengers in the whole of this carriage. So we can sit where we like. Nobody's going to catch us, OK!' He slid back the first class door with a flourish. 'Now, after you!'

Brian was first to step inside. 'Wow,' he breathed, as he gazed around the old compartment.

The seats in the carriage were deep and squashy and upholstered in red, velvety fabric. The walls were panelled with rich walnut and even the luggage rack was inlaid with polished wood.

'*This* is the life,' said Brian, sinking into his seat with his hands behind his head.

There was a *clonk*, as Craig fiddled with a catch beneath the window and released a small folding table. He pulled at a wooden toggle. The blind snapped back into its housing with a crack.

'Amazing!' Emily said.

'Told you it was a good idea,' Brian said.

She smiled and leaned her head against the velvet headrest. 'OK, I admit it. You were right. It was an excellent idea.'

Excellent. Brian smiled. That was just how he felt at this moment. He was riding first class on a train beside his two best mates and soon he would be sitting in the stadium watching his team fight for the cup.

Suddenly, Brian sat bolt upright in his seat. He motioned to the others to be quiet. 'Did either of you hear that?'

'Hear what?' asked Craig.

'Music or something,' said Brian. 'I swear I heard something.'

Brian, Craig and Emily stopped talking for a

moment and listened intently. There it was. A creepy, high-pitched tune.

'You mean that kind of whistling?' said Craig, chewing his lip uncertainly.

Brian nodded. By now, the unmistakable sound of whistling was drifting up the corridor towards them.

'Who do you think it is?' Craig said. 'Do you think it's an inspector?'

'I think I'm going to be sick,' said Emily, closing her eyes.

Brian tried to find some words of reassurance but failed. The thin, reedy notes echoing through the corridor reminded him of nasty, old-fashioned, wind-up jack-in-the-box tunes. He gave an involuntary shudder as he thought back to the brightly painted jack-in-the-box he'd been given for his fourth birthday. It had made him hate clowns for ever afterwards. Other kids were afraid of the dark but Brian hated that clown – the way it would jump out, its face leering – along with that slow and awful tune. He glanced around. Even Craig looked fearful.

Brian didn't know why but that whistling was creeping him out.

The whistling sounded like it was just outside in the corridor.

He glanced through the window and his blood froze. There, reflected in the long carriage window, was the ticket inspector. From the angle where Brian was sitting, he could see that the inspector was still a little way down the main carriage, but he would be coming closer very soon.

Craig and Emily seemed to see him at the same moment.

'He's almost here!' hissed Craig. 'What shall we do?'

'Quick,' Brian whispered, searching desperately round the carriage. 'Hide!'

'But there's nowhere to hide . . . we're trapped!' Emily said. 'There's only one way out and that's into the corridor.'

'We're done for,' hissed Craig, panicking.

They all heard the slow, heavy footsteps making their way up the corridor towards their compartment, accompanying the eerie whistling.

Brian's eyes desperately scanned the small compartment in vain, trying to find a safe place to hide. The sound of the inspector's shoes on the hard corridor floor grew louder.

In desperation, Brian dived for the floor. 'Quick,' he urged. 'Get as low as you can and press yourselves up against the door. Hopefully he'll look in but not down.'

'I told you this was a terrible idea,' whispered Emily angrily. 'We should have bought a ticket. Now he'll chuck us off the train.'

Craig groaned. 'It's miles. It'll take us *ages* to walk.'

Brian was silent. Skipping the fare had seemed like a bit of a lark when he'd come up with the idea earlier. He'd actually not considered that they might get caught. After all, they'd travelled this line dozens of times before and never even seen a ticket inspector.

The footsteps were so close now Brian could feel their vibration through the train floor. The whistling was getting louder and louder. He tried not to think about how there was only a thin sliding door between them and the ticket inspector.

Just then, the footsteps and the whistling stopped.

Brian held his breath as he realized the ticket inspector was right outside the door.

Beside him, Emily and Craig stiffened, and his own mind raced as he tried not to imagine the inspector's face peering in through the compartment window. The silence seemed to stretch on for ever.

Why didn't the man leave? Brian's heart was pounding now. What was taking him so long? It could only mean one thing: he'd rumbled them and any second now they would feel the compartment door slide back and trouble would start.

But suddenly, to Brian's relief, the footsteps started up again. This time, they were heading away from the door towards the front of the carriage. The ticket inspector was leaving. Brian was so grateful he could hardly speak. He looked at his friends in triumph. They had got away with it!

* * *

'Well, we can't stay in this compartment,' said Emily, straightening her football top. 'There's nowhere to hide, and we are bound to get caught. We should go to where the other fans are, or somewhere where it's less exposed.'

'Emily's right,' Brian said, standing up. 'We can't stay here and get caught. We'll have to split up. That way it'll be easier to hide. Then, just before the train pulls into our station, we'll break cover and meet up in the front carriage. You know, the one just behind the driver.'

Emily nodded in agreement. 'I'll head for the guard's carriage where they store the luggage and bicycles and stuff. There's bound to be a place to hide in there.'

'Good idea,' said Brian. 'You go the same way as Em, Craig. I'll stand in the corridor and keep an eye out while you make your move.'

He slid the compartment door back and slipped into the passageway. To his relief it was totally empty. 'Coast's clear,' he whispered. 'But I think you'd better head that way. The guard's carriage is always at the back of the train.'

Emily and Craig disappeared along the corridor whilst Brian's eyes darted nervously from one end of the carriage to the other, checking for danger signs. They'd almost reached the adjoining carriage door when Emily gave him a final glance over her shoulder.

'Go on,' he hissed. 'Just go!'

Without the others, the carriage seemed deathly silent to Brian. His stomach was making knots and he felt completely exposed. He couldn't understand why, but the sound of the whistling and the footsteps had completely unnerved him. It all just felt . . . *wrong*.

Brian gripped the side of the compartment door and took a deep breath. He was just wondering where he could hide when he felt a burst of pain in his fingertip. He snatched his hand away from the panelled door. A splinter of wood poked out from underneath his nail and a small drop of blood oozed in a crimson blob. Brian examined the compartment door carefully. He noticed a set of initials carved into the architrave: **RM.** Brian sucked his finger crossly. It looked as if the letters had been hacked into the frame, probably with a penknife, and they'd left it rough around the edges – that was why he'd caught his finger on it. As he rummaged in his pocket for a tissue, the sound of whistling filled the air once more.

Surely the ticket inspector couldn't be back again already? Brian fixed his eyes on the door. *Wait a minute*, Brian thought. *Wasn't that the same direction the inspector had come from last time? How can that be?* Brian was sure he'd heard him exit the corridor the other way. It didn't make sense.

The whistling was louder now, and Brian felt his mind go into overdrive. Perhaps the inspector had doubled back past their carriage without them noticing? He shook his head. *No, it was impossible.* Craig and Emily had made their escape immediately after the inspector had disappeared from sight.

Whatever the explanation, this wasn't the time to rationalize. He had to find a place to hide, and fast. As quick as a flash, he darted down the corridor and dived into the compartment, pulling the door tightly shut behind him. Once inside, he jumped up on to the seat and scrambled into the only available hiding-place: the overhead luggage rack. It was a tight squeeze, and Brian had to force his way on to the ledge and lie with his nose pressed up against the ceiling. He wondered if he'd ever manage to struggle out again.

The sound of footsteps, slow and heavy, made their way along the corridor towards his compartment, and Brian wished that Emily and Craig were still with him. The footsteps stopped. Once again, the ticket inspector lingered outside the compartment door. Surely the inspector was never going to spot him up here? Brian could feel sweat forming on his forehead. And in that instant, an overwhelming urge gripped him. He wanted to peek – to stare over the edge and get a good look at the man who whistled annoying tunes. The feeling took such a sharp hold of him that before he had time to think about the risk, Brian had slid to the edge of the luggage shelf and craned his neck over the edge.

The ticket inspector was walking away and Brian only managed to catch sight of the back of his head. It was more than enough. Brian threw himself back, tight to the wall, his heart racing. There was only one other person he'd ever seen in his life with that hair – jet-black with a pure white streak down the middle. Badger hair, he'd thought at the time. But it *couldn't* be the ticket seller. It was impossible. He hadn't even left his booth.

As the footsteps drifted away, Brian wondered what to do. Should he go and find Craig and Emily and tell them? They might think that he was being ridiculous. Surely it'd be worth riding out the weirdness – after all, they were only going a couple of stops. But doubts still ate away at him. Things weren't right on this train. Not right at all.

Brian realized he'd become unbearably hot. He

wriggled uncomfortably on the hard wood. It had seemed a good idea at the time, the three of them splitting up, but now he wasn't so sure. The isolation had started to make him anxious, and he was beginning to get angry at being so scared of some old ticket inspector. He had had enough. He decided to go and find Craig and Emily, or at least to find the compartment full of supporters that he had seen from the station earlier.

He struggled down from the luggage shelf and crept into the corridor. Thankfully it was clear. There wasn't another soul in sight, and no noise either. Brian felt a sense of unease. During the whole time on the train, they had all been so preoccupied with getting caught; it had never occurred to Brian that he hadn't seen a single other passenger.

Not one.

Curious, he made his way along the length of the corridor, peering into every compartment along the way.

They were all empty.

'Weird,' he said to himself.

Still, it'll be different in the next carriage, Brian told himself. It had to be. He reached for the handle of the adjoining door, certain that it would be full of football songs and noisy chatter, and he'd see Craig and Emily singing along with everyone else.

He stepped inside and looked around. It, too, was empty.

There was no noise, no litter and no people. Brian was utterly alone. And then he heard something that made him freeze.

The sound of whistling and footsteps.

A lump like a stone rose up in Brian's throat. He willed himself to run but his whole body was bound by terror. As the low, unearthly sound filled the corridor, he somehow felt the cheerful little tune was mocking him. For what seemed like eternity, Brian stood helplessly in the corridor trying to decide which direction the inspector would appear from next. Where could he hide when he didn't even know which way to run?

Brian spotted a door beside him. It was different to the rest, solid from top to bottom with no glass window. He pushed it open and darted inside. He'd managed to find the toilet cubicle – and toilets *always* had locks.

Immediately, he shot the bolt and, stepping backwards, nearly fell over the toilet bowl. Recovering a little, he glanced around him. The room was tiny, the toilet and washbasin swallowing all the available space. He was sure that he could feel the temperature rise, and he was sweating even more, but this time the sweat was cold and clinging.

The ticket inspector was inside the carriage now, Brian was sure of that. He could hear the long, slow footsteps striding along the corridor towards him. They were at odds with Brian's heart, which pumped so fast inside his chest, he worried the inspector might hear.

The footsteps halted outside the cubicle door. The whistling stopped abruptly. *He'll leave in a minute,*

Brian chanted inside his head. *He'll leave in a minute. Please make him leave in a minute.*

Brian watched in horror as the handle began to move. His chest felt suddenly tight and he pulled uncomfortably at the neck of his football shirt.

The handle rattled again, and Brian wedged a foot beneath the door and grasped the lock hard with both hands. It shook violently, but he closed his eyes and held on tight.

And then the pressure on the handle stopped. The whistling and the footsteps receded once more. Brian looked down at his hands – they were red and sore. He slumped on to the toilet seat, wiping his sweaty forehead with the bottom of his shirt.

After a moment, Brian rose shakily to his feet and gathered himself in the mirror. He smoothed down his hair and splashed cold water on his face.

Come on, Magee, he told his reflection, as he stared in the vanity mirror. *What are you so afraid of? The worst he can do is to throw you off the train!*

He took a deep breath and reached for the lock,

but then he pulled his hand away as though the handle were red-hot. The initials RM were carved into the door frame. Brian touched the jagged carving with his fingers. They were rough around the edges, like the ones he'd snagged his finger on in the first class compartment. But when he looked a little closer, he could see that the wood had begun to discolour, which might have meant that the scratches had been done a long time ago.

He wondered briefly who RM was. The carvings reminded Brian of one of those nature trails where the route was carved into stumps along the way. It was almost as if he was following in this RM's footsteps along the train. The thought suddenly made him shiver and he tried to shake it off. Brian reached for the door handle, his mind made up. Being alone on this train was creeping him out way too much. He had to go and find Craig and Emily.

As Brian left the tiny cubicle, he formed a plan. As soon as he found Craig and Emily, they'd stick together and get off the train – even if it wasn't the station they wanted.

But they must have had the same idea as Brian because as he shut the toilet door he heard them behind him.

'Craig, Emily!' Brian yelled. 'Over here!' It was obvious from their pale faces and pinched expressions that something was very wrong.

'I cut my arm,' Emily said.

'How did you do that?' Brian asked.

'It was just now, when me and Craig were making our way towards the front to find you.'

'Yeah,' nodded Craig, his cheeks still pale and shocked. 'We were in the mail carriage down there, when the ticket inspector came. I had to dive behind a parcel sack to get out of his way. I thought he'd seen me, but he just walked past. It was a right heart stopper, I can tell you.'

'And I managed to squeeze between a couple of weird-looking antique bikes,' explained Emily. 'He didn't spot me either but there was a sharp bit on one of the mudguards. It scratched my arm.'

Brian nodded. 'I saw him make his way down there just now. I wondered if you'd manage to get out of the way in time.'

'What about you?' asked Craig. 'Where did you hide?'

'It's a long story, but let's just say the whole thing's weirded me out. The guy just seemed to keep coming and coming and even though I tried to work out which direction I'd last seen him, he always seemed to turn up from the other.'

Emily nodded in agreement. 'And his hair too! Did you see it?'

'With a white stripe down the back,' said Craig. 'Just like a . . .'

'. . . badger,' Brian finished. 'It was exactly the same as the ticket seller's hair back at the station. I remember seeing it.'

Emily stared hard at Brian. 'Surely there can't be two people with such weird hair, can there?'

Craig rubbed his head in agitation. 'Well, we have

to get off, that's all I know. I won't be happy until I've left this train!'

'But that's the whole point,' Emily said anxiously. 'How can we leave, when that man's everywhere?'

'We'll have to take a chance, that's all,' Brian told the others. 'If we stay where we are, it won't be long before he's back.'

'Where are we going?' asked Craig, as he followed Brian's lead.

'To the front carriage,' Brian said determinedly. 'If we're up the front, at least we know what direction he's going to come from. We could always block the door or something.'

Despite his brave words, Brian's heart was thumping out of his chest. 'Coast's clear,' he whispered, trying to hide his relief each time he opened a door.

Eventually, they made it to the front carriage. Like all the others, it was old-fashioned and seemed to be empty. They'd barely had time to close the carriage door when Craig gave a shout. 'We're slowing down!' he cried, rushing towards the sliding window in the carriage door.

Brian felt himself grinning. 'Look,' he said, pointing at a long steel shed beside them. 'That's the engine shed. We must be coming into the station.'

Sure enough, the tarmac of the platform suddenly ran along beside them and Craig gave a whoop of joy. 'Yes!' he shouted in excitement. 'We're going to make it. We're actually going to make it. We are going to get off this train at last! I take back everything I said about you earlier, Magee. You're a genius!'

Emily managed a smile. 'More like lucky,' she said, shaking her head.

'Hang on . . . wait a minute! Listen . . .' said Brian.

Emily looked desperately at him. 'It can't be. Not now!'

The sound of whistling grew suddenly louder, and now they could hear the ticket inspector's footsteps too. The carriage floor felt as though it was rattling with the inspector's footfalls.

'He's just behind the door!' yelled Craig, terrified.

Emily threw her body against the adjoining door and grabbed the handle hard. 'Craig,' she shouted. 'Come and help me hold the door. We'll keep him out until we reach the station, and then we can leg it.'

The handle began to rattle on the other side and Emily and Craig hung on for dear life.

'We're pulling in!' Brian shouted. 'Hold on!' He gave the brass handle on the door a tug.

It refused to budge.

'I don't believe this,' Brian said to himself, and he tried the handle once again.

'Hurry up!' shrieked Emily from the end of the carriage. 'We can't hold him much longer.'

The whistling seemed relentless now. It filled the whole carriage, the shrill melody assaulting Brian's ears, making it hard for him to think. He could see groups of passengers crowding along the platform. Brian began to bang on the glass with both fists. 'Please help us! I can't open the door! We have to get off!'

'What's going on?' yelled Craig, angrily. 'Get that door open!'

'I'm trying!' Brian replied, still banging and shouting. 'But it's stuck fast, so I'm trying to get help.' Nobody on the platform seemed to even glance the way of the train. In fact, nobody took any notice. It was as if they couldn't see him.

Or the train.

'Please,' Emily begged. 'You *have* to get it open, Brian. We can't hold on!'

Suddenly, Brian noticed a small, angular figure seated in the corner. It was an elderly passenger he hadn't noticed until now. It was an outside chance, but perhaps he could help them.

'Excuse me, but we're—'

Brian stopped speaking as he saw for the first time what the man was doing. Brian's eyes moved to the old man's hands and his body trembled. Thin, knotted fingers wielded a penknife. Through the whistling, Brian seemed to be able to hear the scrape of metal on wood as the blade etched a scar into the panelling near where the man sat. Brian saw the deep curves of the letter R already finished. Now the old man was working carefully on the M.

Brian's eyes were locked on that letter. M, he read. M for Magee.

Terror flooded Brian's body. As he looked around, he saw for the first time that the carriage that he, Emily and Craig were in was different to the others. The wooden floor, panelled walls and wooden ceiling were covered in carved letters.

Thousands of carved letters.

All of them read RM.

'U-Uncle Ray?' Brian stammered, hardly daring to believe it. 'Is that you?'

Slowly, the man's wizened cheeks turned to face him and his mouth twisted into a thin smile. 'You should have bought a ticket, son,' he said in a hollow, cracked voice.

Brian's arms fell helplessly to his sides. The carriage was deathly silent as the train picked up speed along the track.

Silent except for a soft, low whistling right behind him . . .

KILLING TIME

Alex Leigh flopped down on her bed and idly thumbed the pages of a magazine.

It was Saturday morning, and Alex's best friends, Emma and Polly, had come round for their usual makeover session. Every week, they would attempt to transform one of themselves into a celebrity from the pages of their favourite magazine.

Emma had got some crimping irons for her birthday and was desperate to try them out. So when

Polly volunteered to be her model, Emma was delighted. She pushed Polly down on to Alex's bedroom stool before she could change her mind and began to grapple inexpertly with the steaming plates. Alex contented herself with the role of stylist. She lay on her tummy, chin in hands, advising Emma and Polly from the comfort of her bed.

'Don't brush it, that's all I'm saying,' Alex said.

'Why not?' Polly asked, wincing slightly as Emma just missed her earlobe with the hot plates. 'Why shouldn't I brush it?'

'Will you just keep still?' Emma said in frustration. 'I've nearly finished. I'm on the fringe.'

'Leave the fringe, Emma,' Alex advised in an earnest voice. 'It's a crimp too far.'

Emma leaned over the top of Polly's head and stared at her. 'Do you think so?'

'I'm sure,' Alex said. She reached over and loaded a CD into her stereo, grabbing a tube of crisps from the dresser. 'Plus it's snack time. Anyone for a cheese and chive Pringle?'

As the CD began to play, Emma unplugged the hair tongs and joined Alex on the duvet. She helped herself to crisps. 'Hey – I love this song! I didn't know you had it.'

Alex grinned. 'You can borrow it if you like.'

They sang along while Polly admired her new look in the mirror. 'It's great, but why did you tell me not to brush it?'

Alex noticed Polly and Emma looking at her and seized her chance. She pushed three crisps in her mouth sideways. 'Because . . .' She stopped as her eyes began to water. 'Because . . .'

'Alex?' said Polly, looking up from the dresser. 'Are you all right?'

But Alex didn't answer. Instead, her eyes widened and her throat began to tighten. She clutched at her chest and began to heave.

'She's choking!' shrieked Emma. 'What shall we do?'

The heaving turned to gasping, and Alex began to grab at the duvet, writhing and jerking. She gave them a desperate look before sliding heavily to the floor.

'Look, look. Her face is turning purple!' Emma shrieked.

Immediately, Polly dropped to her knees and began slapping Alex's shoulder blades hard. 'Quick, Em, bang her on the back!'

The girls watched in horror as Alex slumped downward and lay motionless on the carpet. There was a moment's shocked silence, then they heard footsteps on the stairs outside the door.

The bedroom door rattled and a head appeared.

'Only me, girls. Just to tell you—' Alex's mum stopped mid-sentence. 'Is something the matter?'

Wordlessly, Polly and Emma stood back to reveal Alex's body slumped on the carpet.

'We don't know how it happened, Mrs Leigh,' Emma began. 'We were just . . . crimping, you know . . . and then Alex . . . snacks . . .' Her sentence descended into nothing.

There was an awkward silence, and then someone giggled.

'Gotcha!' Alex said, snapping her eyes open. She clambered to her feet and took a bow.

'Alex!' gasped Polly and Emma at the same time.

'You didn't believe I was really dead, did you?' Alex laughed. 'I was only acting.'

Polly shoved Alex in the arm. 'You scared me, you idiot!'

'Sorry, Pol,' Alex said sheepishly. 'So . . . I guess I got it right, then?'

'That was *awesome*, Al!' Emma said. 'Polly and me . . . well, we thought you really were in trouble.'

'Honestly?' Alex said, glowing with pride. 'Was I really that good?'

'Absolutely,' nodded Polly. 'You had us fooled. My heart's still thumping like mad!'

It was exactly the response Alex had been hoping for, because tomorrow they had drama and their teacher, Miss LaSalle, had promised the class a game of Wink Murder. Straight away, Alex had realized this was the perfect opportunity to impress her. Alex's main ambition was to become a famous actress, and Miss LaSalle had important connections in the showbiz world. She had been an actress herself and even starred in a movie – although it hadn't done very well at the cinema. Every summer Miss LaSalle took two of her most promising pupils to a theatre workshop, where famous actors would come in and do training sessions with them. This year, Alex was determined to be one of those chosen.

Alex smiled and reached for the empty Pringles tube lying on the carpet. 'What can I say?' she began in a fake-Hollywood accent, holding it to her cheek like an Oscar statuette. 'If it wasn't for the support of my friends, and of course my mother's healthy cooking, I wouldn't be accepting this award today . . .'

Mrs Leigh smiled. 'Time to come back to the real world now, Alex. Polly's mum's waiting outside in her car.'

Alex shrugged at Emma and Polly. 'Everyone's a critic.'

After waving Polly and Emma goodbye, Alex followed her mother into the kitchen. '*Because* you're the best mum ever,' she began, 'do you think you might do me a small favour?'

Mrs Leigh looked up from loading the washing-machine. 'Look, Alex, if you want me to wash your jeans, then you'd better hurry up and bring them down to me. This is the only coloured wash I'm doing tonight.'

Alex shook her head. 'No, Mum, it's nothing like that. I just want you to wink at me from time to time.'

Mrs Leigh smoothed a curl from her forehead and frowned. 'You've lost me.'

'Wink. You know.' She gave her a big wink with her left eye.

'Sometimes I wonder about you, Alex,' Mrs Leigh said, reaching for the washing-powder.

'But this is homework, Mum – honestly. It's for drama. We're having a game of Wink Murder tomorrow and I want to make sure I'm totally prepared,' Alex explained.

'Wink Murder?' Her mum tilted her head to one side and stared at Alex, as if to say, 'What are you talking about?'

Alex knew that she'd have to start at the beginning. 'Listen – Wink Murder's a game we play in drama. The whole class sits in a circle and everyone closes their eyes. Then Miss LaSalle picks someone out and taps them on the back.'

'Miss LaSalle?'

'*Yes*, she's our drama teacher,' Alex replied impatiently. 'Anyway, the person she chooses gets to be the murderer, understand? And because everyone has their eyes closed, they don't know who that person is. They just have to wait to be killed.'

Alex's mum shook her head. 'So how does the murderer kill everybody, then?'

'By winking at them, of course,' Alex replied.

'But you've all got your eyes closed. How would you see?'

'We've *opened* them again by now. Try to keep up, Mum. Anyway, if you get winked at – and this is the best bit – you have to die in the most dramatic way possible.'

'And what happens when everyone's dead? It seems a bit of a pointless game to me,' her mum said, turning back to the washing-machine.

'No, you don't understand. It's the detective's job to stand in the middle of the circle and catch the murderer out before he kills everyone in the class.'

'But you didn't say there was a detective.'

Alex was exasperated now. 'OK, so I left that bit out. Miss LaSalle chooses somebody to be a detective at the start of the game.' Alex stopped to take a deep breath. 'But the point is this: we've got drama tomorrow, and I want my death to be the best out of everybody's.'

'Well – if it'll help, then I suppose I can wink at you once in a while.' Her mum gave Alex a big wink.

'Arrgh,' Alex groaned, and collapsed on to the floor.

Despite the fact it was an overcast Monday morning, Alex felt really cheerful. 'I can't wait for drama,' she said to Emma as they made their way towards the school gates.

'I can't wait to see you try out that dying routine on the others – it really shook me up!' Emma replied.

Up ahead, Alex could see Polly waiting for them. She was wearing a big hat.

Alex sighed as she approached Polly. 'You brushed it, didn't you?'

Polly gave her a sheepish look. 'Well – I didn't think that it would be that big a deal . . . but look at what's happened.' She removed her hat to reveal a huge bush of frizzy hair.

'I told you not to, Pol. You're just supposed to comb it through with your fingers or it goes . . .'

'. . . crazy,' finished Polly.

Emma put her head on one side. 'Actually, it's not

that bad,' she said loyally. 'I mean big hair is really in at the moment, isn't it, Alex?'

Alex nodded, trying hard not to laugh.

Polly managed a small smile. 'Really?'

'Absolutely.' Alex avoided her gaze, afraid she might burst out laughing and hurt Polly's feelings. 'Anyway, look on the bright side – it washes out, and it doesn't look nearly as bad as when Emma dyed her hair last year.'

'Hey! I thought that looked pretty cool!' Emma said indignantly. Alex and Polly began to hoot with laughter.

Suddenly, there were footsteps behind them. Alex turned, and she immediately felt her smile fade. It was Christian Francis, a boy with all the charm of a spitting cobra. Alex remembered a time back in Year 7 when she'd tried to be friends with him. Even now the whole thing still made her shudder. He had been nice to her for a while, and Alex had even started to like him. But in a single moment everything had changed.

It was a maths test that did it. Christian hadn't done any revision and insisted on sitting next to Alex so he could copy her work. She'd refused, and that was when she saw the other side of Christian Francis.

First, he stopped talking to her – but that wasn't a problem; Alex could handle that. But then other things started happening. Sick stuff.

Her locker was broken into and her maths book soaked with water. Then the straps on her schoolbag were cut and slashed with scissors. The detention was hard to take, especially when Christian Francis smirked at her through the window. She had told the class teacher what had happened, only to find that she didn't believe Alex's story, and Alex came back to find that her mobile had 'dropped' out of her backpack and the screen was broken. But she could never prove any of it was Christian.

But it had been the rat that disturbed her the most. She'd found it inside her desk, its stinking, rigid little body crawling with parasites, and what looked like maggots. It also looked as though it had been mangled somehow. Alex remembered wondering at the time whether Christian had found it like that . . . or whether he had killed it.

Even the teacher felt queasy as she removed the tiny corpse from Alex's desk. 'Who did it?' she had demanded. 'Which individual in this class is sick enough to do such a thing?'

Nobody had answered, but Christian gave Alex the tiniest of smiles. It was so small that only she noticed.

But it had been enough.

Since then, she had given Christian a very wide berth. Other kids in her class had experienced similar things when they had problems with him, though none of them had ever had anything quite as bad as the rat. Mostly, they'd come back to their lockers to see that the metal doors had been kicked in or written on in thick permanent marker pen. Or sometimes their textbooks were torn to pieces and strewn down the corridor. But Christian was always too clever to get caught. He had one friend – a boy called Adam Moran – who had all the intelligence of a caveman. For some reason that Alex could never quite fathom, he worshipped the ground Christian Francis walked on. Wherever he went, Adam followed with the same inane grin plastered across his stupid face.

More recently, Christian had asked Polly to go with him to the Valentine Disco, but she had said no. Alex had stiffened when Polly had told her. If a trivial thing like a maths test could lead to a dead rat, Alex wondered what a personal knock-back might do.

She watched wordlessly as Christian approached, an uncomfortable feeling rising in the pit of her stomach. Not for the first time, he reminded Alex of a Rottweiler: cruel and tenacious. He gave a lick of his thin lips as he headed towards Polly and in that instant Alex knew there was going to be trouble.

'*Someone*'s having a bad hair day!' he began with a sneer. 'What happened, Polly? Did you get plugged into the mains?'

'Go away, lizard features,' snapped Emma.

Christian gave a dry laugh and ran a hand through his hair. 'You don't *really* mean that, babe.'

'Oh – I think I do,' Emma replied coolly.

Alex shot a look at Polly – she could see that Christian had already upset her.

Christian turned his attention back to Polly. 'So – is this a new thing, then, the Hagrid look? Will you be growing a beard to match and be putting on five stone? Oops, sorry, I can see you've done the weight thing already.' He and Adam laughed loudly.

Polly's face crumpled. Christian really seemed to be enjoying himself. Alex was furious. *How can he be so mean?* Anger began to rise up inside her. Polly was the nicest person she knew – she wouldn't upset anyone. Christian had no right to give her such a hard time just because she wouldn't go on a stupid date with him. Alex decided to take action. 'Right, that's it, I've had enough—'

'Please – just leave it, Alex,' Polly said, grabbing her arm. 'I'd rather forget about it.'

'Yeah, Pol's right, Alex – everyone knows that Adam and Christian are losers,' agreed Emma, her cheeks flushed with anger.

The girls linked arms and headed into school.

'I wouldn't take the main entrance, Polly,' shouted Christian after them. 'Even if your hair fits through, your bum definitely won't!'

Alex watched Polly turn round. *Oh no*, she thought.

'I know *exactly* why you're doing all this,' Polly said evenly. She looked Christian in the face. 'It's because I wouldn't go to the Valentine Disco with you, isn't it?'

Christian shrugged. 'I don't know what you're talking about. I was just being honest about your hair and stuff. No need to get upset.'

But Alex could see Polly was past being upset. She was so angry, she was actually shaking.

'Well, now *I'm* being honest,' Polly went on. 'If you think I'd ever go *anywhere* on a date with a creep like you, then you're deluding yourself.'

Christian staggered back in mock horror. 'Ooh,' he said, gripping his chest. 'I'm wounded. You're killing me, babe.'

Adam guffawed loudly, enjoying the joke. Alex felt like killing him.

But Polly wasn't finished yet. When she spoke again, her voice was like steel. She walked over to Christian and smiled. 'Do you know something,' she said, as cool as a cucumber, 'I nearly said yes to that disco but I realized I didn't know you well enough. In fact, I was going to give it a week and ask *you* to the cinema instead.'

For the first time ever, Alex saw Christian look uncertain. His whole demeanour suddenly changed. If she wasn't mistaken, he looked flattered.

'Really?' he said, his cheeks flushing with pleasure. 'You were going to ask me out?'

Polly put her face close to his and Alex thought for one insane moment that she was going to kiss him on the cheek – but Polly broke off and burst out laughing instead.

'As if!' Polly said with a wicked laugh. 'As if I'd ever go out with someone like you! Unlike you, I'm neither dumb nor desperate!' Polly turned away. 'And by the way,' she said as a parting shot, 'with breath like yours, a mint wouldn't hurt!'

There was a moment's absolute silence. Some Year 8 girls had been passing by, and Alex watched with satisfaction as they pointed and laughed at Christian. His cheeks glowed scarlet with humiliation.

'Pol, that . . . was . . . AMAZING,' said Alex, bursting into laughter.

'Genius, sheer genius!' agreed Emma, grinning widely.

They walked off arm in arm, still laughing. Behind them Christian thumped Adam in the arm and shouted something at them, but it was lost in the chatter of the playground.

Alex couldn't help shuffling impatiently as Miss LaSalle addressed the class.

'Now – as I've told you all before,' she said, 'a good actor never acts. He, or she, merely *reacts.*' Miss LaSalle paused, and made sure that everyone was paying attention. 'Wink Murder may be only a game, but it's also a very worthy exercise in some of the more basic acting skills . . .'

Alex was only half listening. 'I hope I'm not the murderer,' she whispered excitedly.

Emma looked at her. 'Why's that?'

'Can't wink,' replied Alex seriously. She gave Emma and Polly a quick demonstration.

'Pathetic,' giggled Emma. 'That was more like a blink!'

Alex shrugged. 'Happens every time,' she said. 'I've tried practising but I still can't do it. It's like one of my eyelids won't work without the other one.'

Emma grasped her by the shoulders and looked her squarely in the face. 'It's easy,' she said. 'Copy me.'

Polly gave a giggle. 'If you two could see yourselves!'

'Shh,' said Emma. 'This is serious. Right, Al, look me in the eye. Now relax and clear your mind. Try to think about something other than winking.'

'Like what?' asked Alex, who couldn't think about anything *except* winking now.

'I don't know,' said Emma. 'Use your imagination. Now, when I give the signal, just relax and let your eyelid go. Don't give it too much thought, just copy me, OK?'

Alex nodded.

'Great,' said Emma. 'Now on the count of three. One . . . two . . . three . . . wink!'

'How did I do?' asked Alex.

Polly and Emma looked at each other.

'Still a blink, I'm afraid,' Emma said.

'I'd stick to dying if I were you,' said Polly diplomatically.

'Just keep practising,' Emma added. 'If you remember what I've told you, you'll soon be able to give the perfect killer wink!'

'I prefer the dying bit anyway,' shrugged Alex, her mind turning back to the theatre workshop.

'And me,' nodded Polly. 'I can't wait to try out my twitching.'

Alex was puzzled. 'Twitching?'

'Yeah, my brother says that when someone dies, their nerves are still going for ages afterwards. It makes their whole body twitch like crazy, you know, arms, legs and stuff.'

Miss LaSalle clapped her hands together for silence. 'It is time,' she announced, 'for a murderer to be found. Let's move our chairs and put them in a ring.'

Amidst the din of chairs scraping, Christian and Adam approached Alex, Emma and Polly. Alex braced herself for the backlash from Polly's earlier outburst. But considering his earlier humiliation, Christian looked surprisingly calm.

'What do *you* want?' demanded Emma, scowling.

'Girls,' Christian said, holding up his hands in surrender. 'About earlier.' His face was a picture of regret. 'I've been thinking about what you did back there and I just wanted to let you know I understand. I deserved it. I was rude to Polly and it was really out of order.'

The girls eyed each other suspiciously. *This day is getting weirder and weirder*, thought Alex. She'd never heard Christian apologize to anyone, *ever*. Perhaps Polly had got to him after all.

'Polly, I'm *really* sorry I upset you,' Christian continued. He pulled a bag of sweets from his pocket and gave them to her. 'I thought these might help make up for things a bit.'

Emma was the first one of the girls to react. 'It's a trap, Polly. Don't take them.'

Polly hesitated.

'You still don't trust me?' said Christian, looking hurt. 'After I've said sorry and everything.' He opened the bag and popped a sweet in his mouth. 'Look, they're really good, honestly.'

'Well – he seems genuine enough,' whispered Polly to Alex, still hesitating slightly. She turned towards Christian. 'If you really mean it about being sorry and everything, then I suppose it can't hurt.' She reached for a sweet and put it in her mouth.

Christian looked at Adam. They both grinned.

'Nice?' Christian asked, his pleasant expression replaced with a more familiar leer.

'Ugh!' shrieked Polly, her face twisted in disgust. 'It's a pepper sweet – disgusting!' She spat it into her hand.

As far as Alex was concerned it was the final straw. 'Do you know something, Christian?' she said. 'I've had enough of you and your nasty little stunts. It's about time someone taught you a lesson.'

Christian's eyes flashed at her, and at once Alex regretted what she'd just said. She felt a flicker of fear she couldn't explain. Without warning, he leaned close. 'Alex,' he said, his voice soft as a whisper. '*I* am the master at revenge.' He gave her a knowing smile. 'I thought *you* of all people would know that.'

At that moment, Miss LaSalle clapped her hands

for silence. 'When you are *quite* ready, Christian, the wink murders can begin!'

Alex hurriedly took her place in the circle, grateful to join Emma and Polly. She still felt shaky from her run-in with Christian.

'Everyone close their eyes,' Miss LaSalle said.

Alex shut her eyes. The incident with Christian had unsettled her but she couldn't afford to lose her focus now. Not when she'd practised so hard for this moment. She cleared her mind, trying to block out Christian's words. The game was all that mattered now, and Alex prayed not to feel Miss LaSalle's tap on her shoulder. She really, really didn't want to be picked as the murderer or the detective. In the silence, she could make out the ticking of the large chrome clock on the wall.

Miss LaSalle's voice broke the silence. 'Everyone – open your eyes.'

Alex breathed a sigh of relief. She hadn't felt a touch on her shoulder. It wasn't going to be her. Beside her, Polly opened her eyes and leaned in to Alex.

'Look who Miss LaSalle's chosen for detective,' she whispered.

Alex turned to the figure in the middle of the circle. A tall, gangly girl with greasy brown hair and bottle-rim glasses stood there, looking as if she wanted the ground to swallow her up.

'Not *Theresa,*' Alex heard Christian say under his breath. 'With her eyesight, we'll all be dead on the floor within a minute. Of all the people to choose! The only one who would have been worse is Polly!'

Alex looked pointedly at Christian. 'You are *such* a pig.'

'That's an insult to pigs!' Emma chimed in.

'Thanks, girls,' Polly said, but Alex could see that Christian was really beginning to get to her. Alex squeezed Polly's arm and smiled. She gave her a wink. 'Chin up, Pol. He'll get bored with it soon – he is so immature.'

'I'll try,' said Polly. Then she laughed. 'Hey, Alex, you know what just happened then, don't you?'

Alex looked blank.

'You winked at me.'

'Did I?' said Alex in surprise. She hadn't even noticed.

'Just wait until I tell Emma,' said Polly. 'She'll never believe me.'

'It is time for the game to begin,' Miss LaSalle continued, with a dramatic arm motion. 'Now – we need complete silence. Theresa, good luck, and mystery murderer, good luck. Now begin.'

Nothing happened for quite a while, although Alex couldn't help gripping the sides of her chair in anticipation. *Please let it be me*, she thought, her mind suddenly buzzing with pictures of herself at the theatre workshop being taught by famous actors. Suddenly, Tim Lawton dived off his chair and fell clumsily to the floor. Alex groaned in dismay. She was going to have to wait for her moment. The first victim of the mystery murderer had been claimed.

Pitiful, thought Alex. *He could've at least put a little bit of effort into his death*. She could see him peeping and smiling when he was supposed to be a lifeless corpse.

But on the bright side, if they were all going to be that useless, Alex would have no competition – she would definitely be the best! She glanced sideways at Polly, only to see that she was unusually quiet, and very pale. 'Are you all right?' Alex mouthed.

Polly nodded weakly. 'I'm fine.'

Alex wasn't convinced. 'Are you sure?' She put her hand on Polly's. It was freezing.

Miss LaSalle stared pointedly at her. 'When you've finished, Alex . . .'

'Sorry, Miss,' Alex said, and returned to the game. She stared everybody out in the circle, hoping to catch the murderer's wink, but to her frustration, she saw nothing. Nobody so much as blinked. Across the circle, a sudden coughing broke the silence. Greg Coulton raised a hand to his throat and gave a strangled, choking cry. Alex watched as Theresa whirled about helplessly, but it was too late – another victim was dead, and the murderer hadn't been caught.

This time, Alex was far more impressed. Greg was

certainly giving it his all; in fact, his death was going on and on and on. He was on his knees, choking and flailing about wildly. It was certainly more entertaining than Tim's pitiful effort.

Alex fidgeted in her chair. *Why didn't the murderer hurry up and strike again?* She waited, exchanging glances with everyone. But still nobody winked. Alex didn't have a clue who the murderer was.

She turned to Polly, hoping she might know where the killer was, but her friend was staring steadfastly into the centre of the circle, refusing to look round. Alex reached out a hand and gave her a tap on the leg. Polly's brown eyes glanced momentarily at her before rolling back into her head and then snapping tightly shut.

Not you too, groaned Alex inwardly.

But Alex was stunned at how good Polly's performance was. Of the people who had 'died' so far, she was by far and away the best. Polly had scrambled off her chair, and stood hunched over, fighting for breath. Alex thought that a real asthmatic would have had a hard time competing with this performance. Suddenly, she sank to her knees, clutching at Alex on the way down. Alex waited for the twitching to start. She was desperate to see how Polly did it. But it looked like her friend had abandoned the idea. Instead, her nails dug harder and harder into Alex's leg.

'OK, Pol,' whispered Alex. 'Stop now – ouch! You're hurting me!' She prized Polly's nails from her thigh and lowered her gently down. As she did so, she noticed her friend's hand felt cold and clammy.

For what seemed like hours, Polly continued to retch and shiver. Fear grew in Alex as white spittle began to froth around her friend's mouth. She heard the class gasp around her as Polly continued to writhe and jerk. Her performance was terrifyingly convincing. Everyone in the class fell silent as their eyes fixed themselves expectantly upon the limp body on the floor. But Polly didn't move. Even her chest was still. There was no rise and fall of breath, not even a flutter. Alex's stomach tightened as a terrifying thought formed in her mind.

Someone in the class spoke. 'Come on, Pol, stop pretending and get up.'

There was no response.

'She's not pretending!' whispered Alex, in a husky voice.

'What did you say?' asked Emma, her voice trembling.

Alex's voice began to rise. 'I said, she's not pretending! Polly's in trouble.' Everyone's faces, including that of Miss LaSalle, seemed stuck in a horrific photograph – no one was moving.

'What are you all waiting for?' Alex screamed. 'Somebody get an ambulance NOW!'

She heard a sob behind her as someone in the class started to cry, but Alex wasn't worried about anyone except Polly. She dived to the floor and cradled her friend's head. 'You're going to be OK, Pol – you'll be fine.' But there was no sign on Polly's face that she understood what Alex was saying. Hot tears spilled from Alex's eyes and splashed against the cheek of her prone friend.

Suddenly the entire room seemed to erupt. Miss LaSalle came to her senses, sending Tim Lawton off to phone for an ambulance.

'Tell them it's an emergency!' she shouted after him.

Alex saw his shocked face disappear down the corridor and prayed for him to hurry. She was dimly aware of Emma chasing after him, anxious to help. All around her children sobbed or stood quietly in groups, their faces white with shock. But Alex never left her best friend's side.

'Come on, Pol,' she begged. 'Hang on in there, *please*!'

But as the sound of sirens filled the air, Polly's lips were already going blue.

Then Alex felt hands on her arms, lifting her away from Polly. 'She will be all right, won't she?' she asked the paramedics. A wave of nausea washed over her as she watched two brightly jacketed ambulance men begin to work to resuscitate Polly.

In her heart, Alex knew the truth. It was too late. Polly was dead.

In the playground, Alex clung tightly to Emma, her body racked with sobs. All she could think about were the paramedics still inside the studio working on poor Polly's body. Alex was so distraught, she barely noticed Emma's tears soaking the sleeve of her sweatshirt.

'This can't be happening,' Alex whispered through her sobs. 'I mean . . . she looked a bit pale when the game began, but she told me she was fine.'

'And I thought the wheezing and stuff was all part of her act,' gulped Emma, her cheeks red and blotchy with tears. 'If only she'd said something at the beginning – told us she didn't feel well. Then we could've done something earlier.'

'We might have saved her,' whispered Alex, tears sliding down her face once again. She closed her eyes, remembering the screams of her classmates as Polly slumped to the floor. Everyone had cried as they'd left the drama studio, even the boys. The only one who'd seemed unruffled was Christian Francis. His face was a mask of calm as he passed her in the corridor.

Alex looked at Emma. 'What on earth are we going to do now, Em?'

But Emma only shook her head, silent tears streaking her face.

Alex bit her lip hard. She felt so *useless*. Inside the doorway, the two paramedics appeared, talking earnestly with the headmaster.

'Come on,' Alex said, wiping her eyes and pushing her way through the murmuring crowd. 'I want to know what they're saying.'

'. . . no obvious signs that we can detect at the moment,' the first paramedic was explaining.

The headmaster looked grave. 'You mean you have no idea at all what caused Polly's death?'

'Not without a post-mortem, I'm afraid,' the paramedic replied.

The headmaster turned to Miss LaSalle who was

standing nearby. Alex could see that her skin looked grey, and she was shivering. 'I think that under the circumstances, the school should have the rest of the day off.' But Alex didn't want time off. Time off wasn't going to bring Polly back. She wanted to find out exactly what it was that had killed her friend.

Alex and Emma wandered home together, trying hard to make sense of it all.

'Why wouldn't they let us stay?' Alex said crossly. 'Surely the police would want witnesses, and we were the ones who knew her best.' She kicked a crumpled hamburger carton lying on the pavement. 'I mean, what's the good of being at home?'

Emma nodded, looking miserable. 'I still can't believe it's happened. Polly was always so healthy. I can't even remember the last time she was off school sick.'

'That's what I mean,' agreed Alex. 'There *has* to be a reason why she suddenly collapsed like that.

Whatever caused her death must have happened at school!'

'Not necessarily,' Emma replied slowly. 'I saw a documentary last week called *Killer Diseases, the Hidden Enemy*. Did you watch it?'

Alex shook her head.

Emma continued. 'Well, according to the programme, sudden deaths happen quite a lot. They're caused by viruses lying dormant in the body. People go on for years without any symptoms at all but then one day, something can just trigger the disease and when it does, well . . .'

Alex shuddered at the thought. She didn't like the idea of Polly having had anything horrible like that. 'It doesn't seem very likely, Emma. I mean, I've never heard of it.'

'It happens,' Emma said earnestly. 'I reckon it's one of those killer diseases that's to blame. After all, if the paramedics don't know what caused it, then what other explanation is there?'

'I don't know. Maybe it was an allergy or

something.' But Alex racked her brain, and couldn't think of one thing that Polly was allergic to. Suddenly, her legs buckled and she had to sit down on the rockery wall of a neighbour's garden. Her head began to spin, and she fought nausea as her temples throbbed and pounded. Emma managed to get her to walk the last few steps to her own front door.

Alex's mum opened the door to the two girls, and immediately helped Emma get Alex into a chair.

'What's happened, Al?' she asked.

'Polly's dead!' Alex said, bursting into uncontrollable sobs. Emma stood by, her eyes trained on the lounge carpet.

'Dead? What do you mean, Alex? Is this some kind of joke?'

Alex threw herself into her mother's arms. 'I wish it was. I *really wish* it was. She just collapsed in drama . . . and that was it. She never got up again.'

'I'm going to go home,' Emma murmured. 'Take care, Al – call me if you need anything.'

'Thank you, Emma,' said Alex's mum faintly. 'But wouldn't you like me to drive you? After all, you've both had a terrible shock.'

But Emma shook her head, fighting tears. 'I think the walk will do me good, if you don't mind, Mrs Leigh.'

Alex's mum nodded. Alex couldn't even say goodbye to her friend. She felt as though her mouth were sealed, and that if she tried to talk to Emma, she might be sick.

It took until supper for Alex to feel calmer. Her mum took her by the hand and led her up to her room. 'Why did it have to happen to someone like Polly, Mum?' she asked, as her mother tucked down the bedcovers.

Mrs Leigh looked sadly at Alex and shook her head. 'I wish I knew the answer, love, really I do. All I can say is that sometimes, life can be very unfair. We can't always control the things that happen.'

'But if I'd acted sooner, Mum, Polly might still be here.'

'You don't *know* that, Alex,' her mum said, stroking her hair. 'No one can say that for sure. Polly was almost certainly a very sick girl. There might not have been anything even doctors could have done.'

But later that night, Alex was still wide awake. Despite her mother's words, she still searched for answers. All she knew was that Polly was OK before school. There had to be something that happened afterwards to change all that. But what?

She listened to her parents talking downstairs in low, worried whispers. Every time her lids grew heavy, images of Polly's blue lips and lifeless body flooded her mind and haunted her dreams. She buried her head into her pillow, trying to shut out the image of Polly's brown eyes staring out at her.

It was the next day, and Emma joined Alex at the school gate. Her eyes were raw and red-rimmed. They said 'Hi' to each other, but neither had the stomach for conversation. As they entered the playground, Alex saw Christian standing in a corner, with a group of younger kids surrounding him. She felt a knot tighten in her stomach. As she approached, her knot was replaced by disbelief. He was telling every detail about Polly's death.

'. . . her eyes were bulging and rolling around in her head . . . and that was when the choking started.' Christian clutched at his throat and began to gag. 'Then all this foam and blood and stuff spewed out of her mouth . . .' he collapsed on to the bench and began writhing about, '. . . and she was doing all this wriggling and jerking like an electric eel or something . . .'

'Gross,' squealed a girl, hiding her face behind her hands. 'Did you *actually* see her die?'

Christian sat up. 'Oh yeah, and I was the one who gave her the kiss of life and called the paramedics. But it was too late . . .'

Alex put her hands to her ears, unable to listen to any more. She burst through the crowd, angry tears streaking her cheeks. 'You're one sick individual, Christian Francis,' she said furiously. 'Why lie to everyone? You didn't try to save Polly, you hated her. In fact, you're probably glad she's dead . . .'

There was an uncomfortable silence before Adam Moran appeared beside Christian. 'Well – I reckon she was poisoned.'

Christian shot him an angry look. 'Don't be stupid. *Of course* she wasn't poisoned.'

'But what about the frothing and stuff?' Adam persisted. 'Rats do that when you poison them.'

'Adam, just shut up,' warned Christian. 'It wasn't poison, OK.'

'Oh, and you know better?' Alex challenged. 'Now you're a paramedic, as well as an idiot.'

In a second, Christian had grabbed Alex by the arm – hard.

'Get off me, you jerk – that hurts!' Alex fumed.

She could feel Christian's breath on her cheek as he whispered in her ear, 'I would keep your mouth shut if I were you, Alex Leigh. You've messed with me before and look where that got you.'

'Pig!' spat Alex, gritting her teeth. 'Polly messed

with you too, Christian, so what did you do to her?'

Suddenly she felt Emma dragging her away. 'Come on, Alex. He's not worth it.'

Alex rubbed the top of her arm and glared at Christian. His smile was fleeting but it was the same one she'd seen on his face that day the rat had been found in her desk. Her mind recalled how unbothered he had seemed when Polly was dying, and suddenly it troubled her. It was almost as if he'd been expecting it. She remembered the argument he'd had with Polly just before drama and, as Emma led Alex inside, she gave Christian a backward glance. He was still spouting his gory story about Polly's death and Alex wondered, not for the first time, exactly what lengths he would go to for revenge.

'As you all know, a field trip to the animal sanctuary was scheduled for this afternoon, and I feel that it would be a very good idea if it still went ahead,' Miss Wilson said, as all the pupils made their way to their seats. Alex couldn't bring herself to look at Polly's desk.

Miss Wilson went around the room handing out worksheets and Alex realized that she'd be relieved to be getting away from school for the day. As soon as the coach pulled into the gates of the Gables Animal Sanctuary, her mood lifted a little.

The class filed off the bus and assembled by the stables. They were greeted by a prim-faced lady with greying hair. 'Now, everyone,' she said. 'My name is Celia Ambrose, and it's my duty to welcome you all to the Gables Animal Sanctuary today. And indeed, "sanctuary" or protection is precisely what this place is all about. We give refuge and a safe home to the many dogs, cats and other pets that are unwanted or mistreated by their owners.'

Alex, Emma and the rest of the class followed Mrs Ambrose towards one of the barns.

'Now, if you'd like to choose a section to visit, our handlers will be available to answer all of your questions,' Celia Ambrose said. 'Cats are stationed along the walkway, dogs in the middle, and rabbits and smaller pets inside the barn at the end.'

'I'm off to look at the cats,' said Emma. Alex watched as she wandered off with one of the handlers. Alex wasn't a great fan of cats – she had always preferred dogs . . . as had Polly. *No – not now*, she said to herself sternly. She tried not to think about Polly. *Polly would have enjoyed it here, so make the best of it.*

She spent some time looking at the chinchillas in the barn, then made her way into the dogs' enclosure. A couple of kennel hands wrestled fistfuls of bouncing leads. There were pedigrees and mongrels; puppies and older, abandoned dogs with greying whiskers. Alex crouched down in the midst of a shaggy huddle, and immediately a small, scraggy terrier with a white beard tugged at her shoelace and refused to let her pass.

'That's Sonny,' said one of the kennel hands. 'He's a bundle of mischief that one. Came to us last year, just skin and bones, red raw with mange. His owners left him tied up in the yard and barely fed him.'

'Come here, you,' Alex said, bending down to stroke him. Tears pricked her eyes as thoughts of Polly flashed through her mind. But just as she was wiping them away a dark shadow fell across them. She looked up. It was Christian Francis.

'I see you've found a flea-bitten mongrel, Alex,' he said with menace. 'And now I look at you both, I can see you've got a lot in common.'

Alex felt her temper flare, but before she could answer, she heard Sonny begin to snarl. He pulled back his lips and barked angrily at Christian. Alex bent down and scooped the dog up in her arms.

Christian grinned in amusement. 'And he's got your nasty temper too, Alex. Looks like it's a match made in stray heaven.'

'Did you want something in particular?' asked Alex, struggling to keep calm.

'Not really,' said Christian, smirking. 'Although it's

heartening to see you've found another mongrel to follow you round now Polly's gone.'

Alex jumped to her feet in fury. If Sonny hadn't got there first, she didn't know what she might have done to Christian's smug face. But as it was, Sonny jumped from her arms and clamped his teeth around Christian's right ankle. Christian yelled in pain, and tried shaking the small dog loose, but Sonny hung on grimly.

'Get him off me!' Christian said, panicking.

A smile crept across Alex's face. 'He doesn't seem to like you very much.' She gently tugged at the little terrier's collar. Sonny snarled and then let go.

'If that little idiot had scratched my new trainers, there would have been hell to pay,' Christian said to Alex.

'Well, you know what they say,' Alex replied. 'Dogs know who's nice and who's not. It's a sixth sense, apparently.'

'That mutt should have a health warning on it,' he

yelled. 'In fact, if you ask me, it'd be better off being put down!'

Alex looked down at Sonny and, without thinking, winked. She was getting good at winking now, she thought, remembering how impressed Polly had been that day. 'Good boy, Sonny,' she said, patting his head.

She left Christian scowling at Sonny and rubbing his ankle, and went off to find Emma before they had to leave.

On the ride home, Alex watched Christian limp awkwardly up the steps of the bus before taking his place next to Adam. Alex should have felt pleased that Christian had got bitten by Sonny – it was the least he deserved for his behaviour recently – but as she stared at him, he gave her such a smug smile that she felt a tingle of fear.

Alex sat at the kitchen table, and her mum plopped a large cup of tea down in front of her. 'How was your trip?'

'Really good, thanks,' Alex began. 'I met this little

dog called Sonny – he wouldn't leave me alone. Polly would have loved him . . .' She tailed off.

'I'm sure she would have, love,' her mum said, holding Alex's hand from across the table.

'I wanted to bring him home,' Alex said suddenly. 'He'd had such a hard life, Mum. The lady said that Sonny needed someone just like me, who'd give him loads of attention and walk him all the time because his last owners tied him up in their yard and practically starved him.'

'Is this a leaflet about the sanctuary?'

Alex passed over the brochure.

Alex's mum leafed through it for a moment or two. 'How about after supper, when your dad gets home, we pop down there and take a look at this marvellous little dog then?'

Alex could hardly believe it. 'Oh, Mum,' she gasped. 'You won't regret it, I promise.'

'I hope not,' laughed Mrs Leigh.

'Can I phone Emma and ask her to come?' Alex asked.

* * *

Alex could hardly believe her ears. 'Dead?' she said quietly. 'What do you mean, Sonny's dead? I only left him a few hours ago. He was full of life then.'

'Why don't you sit down, love?' Alex's mum said. 'Mrs Ambrose is just about to explain.'

Alex felt numb. She sat down heavily on a chair beside Mrs Ambrose's cluttered desk. 'I can't understand it, that's all.'

'Neither can we,' replied Mrs Ambrose. 'Poor little chap took ill just after your class left. Only ever seen it once before. Starts with terrible wheezing, lungs straining like a pair of bellows. The staff called for the vet, but by the time he arrived, he was gone.' She tapped a pencil against the desk. 'Shocking sight – blue gums and frothing at the mouth. Then his eyes went peculiar, rolling back in his head, and that was that. We're all pretty shaken up, I can tell you.'

Alex was struggling to take this all in. *First Polly and now Sonny!*

Emma put an arm around her shoulders, but Alex

was thinking how Sonny's death seemed to be really similar to Polly's. *Surely it has to be a coincidence?*

Alex looked up. 'Mrs Ambrose, you said you've seen it happen once before?'

'Yes. When I was a girl, I lived on my parents' farm. We had a sheepdog who died in pretty much the same way. The vet said he had been poisoned.'

Alex sat bolt upright. She felt as though she had been electrocuted. 'Poisoned?' she breathed.

'It turned out that he'd been drinking sheep-dip,' Mrs Ambrose said, sadly. 'Such a terrible accident.'

But Alex had stopped listening. She had an awful feeling that what had happened to Polly and Sonny was no coincidence . . . and it certainly *wasn't* an accident.

Emma chattered non-stop all the way home. 'I hardly think that Sonny's death has anything to do with Polly,' she said. 'After all, Mrs Ambrose told us Sonny showed signs of poisoning. He probably ate something he shouldn't have.'

Alex's mind began to sort through the tangled mess of the memories of the last few days. *Hadn't somebody else suggested poison, too?* She thought back to this morning, and her argument with Christian in the school playground. Adam Moran had suggested that Polly had been poisoned. But hadn't Christian immediately dismissed the idea? She rubbed her arm, remembering how he had grabbed at her. And what was it she'd said to him? *Polly messed with you, Christian, so what did you do to her?*

Mr Leigh glanced at her in his rear-view mirror. 'Are you all right, Alex? You're very quiet.'

'Me?' Alex said, her thoughts crystallizing. 'I'm fine.'

It was Christian Francis.

He had murdered Polly.

He had also killed Sonny.

It all made sense! Christian had been with Sonny only minutes before the small dog had collapsed, *and* he had had that run-in with Polly on the morning of her death. Alex felt sick, but at the same time, she felt strangely focused too. Christian *hated* being humiliated – surely revenge on Polly and Sonny was the perfect motive!

Alex tried organizing the series of events leading to Polly's death. Only minutes before the game of Wink Murder had begun, Christian had offered Polly a sweet and she had started getting ill just afterwards. Christian must have done something to the one that he offered Polly, and popped an ordinary one into his own mouth as cover.

Alex was sure that she hadn't seen Christian give Sonny anything to eat . . . but she *had* left them alone together as she went to get on the bus. It couldn't have been that long, but Alex was sure it was long enough for Christian to have slipped the dog something deadly.

He *had* killed them both . . . and he had done it with poison! The only thing Alex now had to find out was how.

* * *

The janitor had barely hung up his coat in the staffroom when Alex arrived in school. She crept down the corridor towards her form room. Looking round the door, she could see that there was nobody in yet – not even Miss Wilson.

Alex hesitated in front of Christian's desk. Under normal circumstances, it would never have entered Alex's head to be rifling through someone else's private possessions. She tried not to think about what might happen if she were caught and steeled herself for what she had to do. *These aren't normal circumstances*, she told herself, *and Christian Francis is* definitely *not a normal boy*.

At first glance, there appeared to be nothing strange. A few assorted books with pictures doodled on the cover, textbooks, three tooth-marked pencils and a half-eaten apple wearing a mouldy overcoat. *Perhaps there's something underneath*, Alex thought. As carefully as she could, she rummaged deeper, but to her disappointment found nothing. Absolutely nothing. Alex felt desperate. *This can't be right*, she thought. *There has to be something*.

'Alex Leigh! What are you doing inside Christian's desk?' demanded a voice from the doorway. Alex felt as though her heart would explode through her chest. It was Miss Wilson, her form teacher.

'Um . . . er . . .' said Alex, panicking. She could feel her cheeks burning. She looked in desperation at the clutter inside Christian's desk. Her eyes fell on a scruffy-looking book with doodles of test tubes on the cover.

Quick as a flash, Alex picked up the book and waved it at Miss Wilson. 'Chemistry book, Miss,' she said. 'Christian said I could borrow it to copy up some notes.'

Alex felt her skin prickle. *That had to be it! Chemistry! There are plenty of poisonous things in a chemistry lab.*

Miss Wilson looked at her for a moment longer. 'Hmm – well, just this once, then. You know the rules, Alex,' she said, plonking an armful of books on her own desk at the front of the class.

'Now go outside until the bell goes, please.'

Instead of going outside, Alex headed for the library. It was double chemistry that morning, and Alex was determined to do some research on poisons before she got there. She kept thinking about Christian's expression at the animal sanctuary – it reminded her of the way he'd looked at Polly just before Polly died. A chill ran down her spine.

Alex frantically trawled the Internet for clues. She had to find out what poisons Christian might have taken from the science lab. She glanced anxiously up at the clock – there were only a few minutes until registration, and then chemistry.

She hit the search engine button for what felt like the hundredth time, and suddenly something was there, right in front of her on the screen. A chill ran down her spine, an icy hand gripping the back of her neck.

'Arsine's Manganese: if taken internally causes constriction of the airways, blue lips, convulsions, frothing of the mouth

and, if taken in large enough quantities, death. This can be found in commercial businesses, and laboratories.'

Arsine's Manganese.

Alex was *sure* she'd seen it in the school chemistry lab. The lesson bell sounded, and she made her way to the classroom, slipping Christian's book back into his desk before anyone else arrived. Alex's heart thumped against her chest as she considered her options. She could wait for Christian to make a move, and catch him stealing poison. But that left too much room for error. What if Christian didn't try anything this week? How would she actually prove it? It would be like the rat scene all over again. No proof. She tried not to think about what might happen then. No, there *had* to be another way. She had to remove the poison altogether.

The class filtered into the chemistry lab and Alex took her regular seat. To her frustration, she found Emma leaning across the Bunsen burners, arguing with Christian. He was smirking, with Adam Moran at his side.

Alex saw Emma point at Christian. 'You need a licence to bring toxic waste like you into school.'

Christian's face clouded. 'You ought to watch that mouth of yours, Emma,' he said. 'It's going to get you in serious trouble.'

At that moment, Mr Malone, the chemistry teacher, entered the room.

'Now then,' he said, shrugging on a worn laboratory jacket. 'I need somebody sensible to help me distribute the chemicals for today's experiments.'

It was just the opportunity Alex needed, and before he could do up his buttons, she was at his side. 'I'll help, Mr Malone,' she said.

He accompanied her to the cupboard at the rear of the room that contained all the dangerous chemicals. 'We'll be studying oxidization today,' he said, with a jangle of keys, 'so we'll need a pot of nails.'

Alex's eyes scanned the shelves. There it was!

Arsine's Manganese. It was on the third shelf, beside the Tupperware container of iron nails. For a second, she considered stealing it. She only had to pop it in her pocket and it would be out of Christian's reach. But what would she do afterwards with a bottle of poison? It might do the water supply harm if she put it down a sink, or she might end up getting caught. And then another solution popped into her head – the only permanent solution Alex could think of. She reached across and grabbed the plastic box full of nails, making sure she gave the bottle of poison a sharp knock at the same time. It flew across the shelf and smashed to pieces on the tiled floor.

Mr Malone threw his hands up in fury. 'That was the only bottle of Arsine's Manganese we had, and it's very expensive to replace! Honestly, Alex, I thought you could be trusted.'

'Sorry,' Alex replied. 'I'll help you clean it up.' But she wasn't sorry – she felt relief flooding through her.

'No, you will *not* clean this up,' Mr Malone said.

'This stuff is poisonous. You'll have to fetch the janitor – he's got the proper equipment to clear it up safely.'

Smiling to herself, Alex made her way to the door. On the way, she couldn't help but give Christian a triumphant glare. Oddly, Christian appeared completely unconcerned about the whole incident. He was more interested in trying to light the end of his pencil with a Bunsen burner. Alex could feel a frown clouding her face. *Surely Christian should have been furious with her?* She'd just destroyed his poison, and he didn't seem bothered at all.

She made her way towards the janitor's office feeling more and more confused. For the first time, she began to seriously doubt what she had believed about the poison. Perhaps Christian hadn't poisoned Polly and Sonny after all. Perhaps he'd used another method. Or, even worse, perhaps he'd had nothing to do with any of it. She went over and over the events of the last couple of days as she walked down the corridor. It *had* to be Christian. After all, who else had had the opportunity to do it? Apart from him, there had only been Alex herself who'd been with them before they'd collapsed and died.

She knocked on the janitor's door and explained what had happened. He gathered his mops and buckets and made for the chemistry lab.

All of a sudden, Alex felt worn out. The deaths of Polly and Sonny must have affected her more than she knew, because she was exhausted, and it was only the first lesson of the day. On her way back to class, she made for the girls' toilets so that she could get herself together.

She splashed cold water on her face and tied her hair back into a ponytail. 'Well,' she said to herself, 'you've done everything you can.' Things now seemed a million miles away from the normality of the week before. She gave herself one last tidy-up in the mirror over the washbasin, and winked at herself in the mirror. Alex was getting good at it now. And then she stopped and stared at herself again.

A wink.

That's how the whole thing had started! With a dumb old game of Wink Murder. The game, the drama course – it was all so meaningless now, yet it had seemed so important at the time.

Her footsteps echoed in the corridor as she hurried towards the classroom. But since leaving the toilets, Alex's chest felt tight, and her breathing had become laboured. Perhaps it was the anxiety of what had happened, or it could even be her imagination, she reasoned to herself as she walked on.

But it was getting worse.

Alex was struggling for air, and she began to feel incredibly light-headed. She could actually *feel* her eyes rolling back into her head. In terror, she desperately reached for the door handle to the chemistry lab, but instead, her legs crumpled beneath her. It felt as though a large weight had been dropped on her, driving all the air out of her lungs. She began to feel her body jerk and writhe. There was nothing she could do to stop it.

It was at that moment that the terrible truth of who had *really* killed Polly and Sonny came to her.

It wasn't Christian Francis.

It was her.

As Alex's chest came to a standstill, snapshots flooded her brain. She pictured herself giving her best friend Polly a friendly wink in drama just before the game had started and again, winking at Sonny for biting Christian's ankle. Finally, as death wrapped its fingers around her throat, Alex recalled winking at her own reflection.

Too late, Emma's words came back to haunt her: *'If you remember what I've told you, Alex, you'll soon be able to give the perfect killer wink . . .'*

Terrify yourself with more books from Nick Shadow's
Midnight Library

Vol. I: *Voices*

Kate knows that something is wrong when she starts hearing voices in her head. But she doesn't know what the voices mean, or what terror they will lead her to . . .

Vol. II: *Blood and Sand*

John and Sarah are on the most boring seaside holiday of their lives. And when they come up against the sinister Sandman, they really begin to wish they'd stayed at home . . .

Vol. III: *End Game*

Simon is a computer addict. When he's sent a mysterious new game, the lines between virtual reality and real life become terrifyingly blurred . . .

Terrify yourself with more books from Nick Shadow's
Midnight Library

Vol. IV: *The Cat Lady*

Chloe never quite believed her friend's stories about the Cat Lady. But when a dare goes horribly wrong, she finds out that the truth is more terrifying than anyone had ever imagined . . .

Vol. VI: *Shut your Mouth*

Louise and her mates love to get their sweets from Mr Webster's old-fashioned shop, but when their plan to get some of the new 'Special Delights' goes wrong, could they have bitten off more than they can chew?

Vol. VII: *I Can See You*

Michael didn't want to move out of the city in the first place. And wandering round the countryside in the dark really isn't his idea of fun – particularly when he finds out how dangerous the dark can be . . .